THE
COMMUNIST'S
DAUGHTER

THE COMMUNIST'S DAUGHTER

AROA MORENO DURÁN

Translated from Spanish
by Katie Whittemore

TINDER
PRESS

First published in Spanish as *La Hija Del Comunista* by Caballo de Troya, Penguin
Random House Grupo Editorial in 2017

First published in Great Britain in 2021 by Tinder Press
An imprint of HEADLINE PUBLISHING GROUP

1

ACCIÓN CULTURAL
ESPAÑOLA

Support for the translation of this book was provided by Acción Cultural Española, AC/E

Cataloguing in Publication Data is available from the British Library

Trade Paperback ISBN 978 1 4722 6898 3

Typeset in Sabon by CC Book Production
Printed and bound in Great Britain by Clays Ltd, Elcograf S.p.A.

HEADLINE PUBLISHING GROUP
An Hachette UK Company
Carmelite House
50 Victoria Embankment
London EC4Y 0DZ

www.tinderpress.co.uk
www.headline.co.uk
www.hachette.co.uk

For Gregorio and Pablo Ulises,
borders to the North and South

He knew what bridges know: they link
above water what
is linked underwater

But one bank was swamp,
the other fire.

Reiner Kunze

KATIA ZIEGLER UNCAPS THE NICKEL-PLATED fountain pen she has used to sign every important document in her life. The one she brought to her wedding in the seventies. All those strange faces in the pews. She remembers he smiled the whole time, but can't recall the features of his face. As if they have been erased at some point in the distant past, and all that's left is the simple fact of his smile. A single image from that time, a snapshot: his back against the silver car, hands in his pockets, a lock of blond hair over his left eye.

October. The rain falls outside, a limp cascade clapping slowly on the roofs. The same rain that would leave them without electricity, and the reason her father had kept a cache of candles and matches. He'd got hold of a flashlight eventually: a replica of the ones the police use, he told them. But the girls liked to play with it at night and it was never on hand when the power went out.

The rainwater unleashes the smell of earth, of the garden. Out of the window, the horizon is close. A neighbour appears, the tidy patio, a man sweeping the street. In the early days, she had taken a picture of the trees every month, witnessed the changing colours while she made the coffee. The rain reminds her of that brown horse and its cold muzzle too. Of sitting on the ground, soaked to the bone. Of the river. The rings of water that met and disappeared. Once, in another October, she planted a hundred bulbs throughout the whole garden. The green broke through and lifted the red clay of the earth. But all of that is in the past now. Asleep. Until the heat starts to close in and all will explode in yellow again.

October. The month of the revolution.

After the rains comes the winter.

When snow falls, it doesn't make a sound.

The East

It had already been dark for hours by the time Papa came through the door. What happened here? he said. You tell me, Mama replied. The cramped space that was our living room, kitchen and bedroom was filled with smoke. Papa grabbed my hands and saw my small fingers were covered in soot. He rubbed his rough fingertips against mine and squeezed hard.

We always spoke with Mama in Spanish and in German with Papa. We didn't ask ourselves why. Papa had learned German in the factory, in Dresden, but he never managed to speak it well. He would sit with Martina and me while we did our assignments and slowly he learned about proper declension, the verb at the end. Hopeless! How will I know what they're trying to say if I don't know the verb, if I don't know what's happening until they're done speaking? In time, he grew used to the language, but though he always managed to communicate, I never really understood everything he said. Papa's German. This language is inhuman, so many letters one after the other, he would complain. Mama refused to learn, and even though Papa left little slips of paper in every room with the names of things – *Fenster*, *Topf*, *Bett*, *Ofen* – she never put a sentence together. She communicated with gestures, a few words. *Kartoffeln*, a kilo, taking off her glove, waving her finger in the shopkeeper's face while Martina and I rolled on the floor in laughter. Just wait, she'd say, you'll have daughters and they'll laugh at you too.

That bitter night, the soup simmered over the fire, the murmur of the radio stirring the air. Papa left the bedroom where he and Mama had been talking since he arrived, talking a long time. Mama went straight to the bathroom and, when she came out, I knew she had been crying. It's the steam, she said. And stirred the pot, the bitter stench of cabbage mixing with the smoke.

I don't want cabbage, it's slimy.

Well, it's what we have.

But we ate it yesterday too.

Martina, I would like to roast you a leg of lamb, I really would, but there aren't any lambs here because it's too cold.

Lambs don't get cold because they have wool. Right, Papa?

Oh, Manuel, for the love of God. Turn that noise off.

The radio was playing the nightly broadcast of the Lipsi, that prudish music the Government used in their attempts to combat rock-and-roll. *Heute tanzen alle jungen Leute Im Lipsi-Schritt, nur noch im Lipsi-Schritt. Alle hat der Takt sofort gefallen. Sie tanzen mit, im Lipsi-Schritt.* Papa turned up the volume and swayed around the room, moving his shoulders, his arms by his hips, little steps, to the right, to the left, forward and back, his eyes half-closed, smiling. He came up behind our mother and untied her apron. Mama turned away, I'm not in the mood, but she couldn't escape his arms. Come on, *mujer*. Pretend it's a *copla*.

They danced until the end of the song. Martina and I watched in astonishment, our pens suspended over our papers, something warm creeping through our bodies and a blue ink stain spreading between the lines of the pages. That's enough, Mama said, enough of this circus, let's eat.

Papa stuck his fingers in the pot and pulled out an almost transparent piece of cabbage. Do you know what this is, girls? A slice of *jamón serrano*. It's delicious, Katia. Do you want some?

Yes.

And you, Martina?

What's *jamón serrano?*

Papa ignored the question. No, Martina? Fine then.

That yellow apartment. Once, I peeled away the wall-paper under the bed and discovered eight different layers, at least. As if every person who'd lived in that fourth-floor garret had wanted to leave their mark, fix their life to those walls, and the next one had tried to cover it up, paper over paper. To reach our stairwell, you had to cross an interior courtyard and its small, anarchic grouping of trees They really ought to paint the walls, Mama would say, it looks like the war's still on. The building was grey. All the buildings were grey back then, grey and peeling, skeletons sheathed in a dirty dress. I hardly had memory of any other home but that apartment, where it was always cold. Papa had introduced us to the neighbours, and we would stop on each landing and watch the people in the building across the way. We made a game out of monitoring their routines: Frau Zengerle, always staring into a pot of water on the stove, Ekaterina reading by the window. When Herr Schmidt died we knew right away, the day he wasn't there waving from his window, tiny glasses slipping down his nose. Something's wrong, Papa said. Later, they told us that, as we watched his window through the chestnut trees, Herr Schmidt – who, after the second war, had never wanted to set foot outside again and scraped by on the meals and solidarity of the neighbouring women – lay on the floor, asleep for eternity.

In the earliest days of living there, we used to wake to the sweet smell of the bakery downstairs. The pipe from the oven ran up the corner of the building to just below our window. But the bakery closed in 1962, along with almost every other business on our street. We always owned very little. In the living room, just a dark wooden table and four chairs; an uneven, unstable shelf – not to be touched – with four plates and four glasses; Papa's books; a narrow bed; a sofa. In the bathroom, a hairbrush with traces of cologne, a thin bar of soap, and Papa's shaving things. In the mornings when I was little, I would sit on the toilet seat, feet dangling, and watch him daub his face with the small brush. Sometimes he would turn to me, bearded in foam, and joke, who am I now? A fat gnome, Papa! And he'd crouch down and rub his nose against mine, smearing it white. The smell of mildew. When we'd first arrived, Mama had washed the green tiles with boric acid and stripped the shine. They're even uglier now, she'd said. But clean, Papa replied. Then there was our parents' room: their bed, under which we were forbidden to play, or even look; a nightstand made of two stacked boxes covered with a small piece of embroidered cloth; a wardrobe. And two prized possessions we babied as if they were living creatures: the radio and the stove. Our winters depended on the proper care of each.

The only window to the outside looked out over a razed block. War destroys everything, Papa said. He often stood silently at the window, as if he wanted to see beyond the snow, beyond the only trees left standing, beyond the night. The war was a ghost. A white stain. Something that happened long ago and which I couldn't quite imagine, even though we all still breathed the ashy air and children played in unused trenches. I hope you never see war, Mama would say. Not my daughters, said Papa, and would tell her to be quiet, change the subject.

We held our hands over the bowl and ate the soup in little sips. Papa blew on his spoon, whistling. Later, our mother boiled linden leaves, burned her right wrist straining the tea. Papa rushed to the bathroom, spread toothpaste on her skin. He held her hand against his lips for a long time, his eyes on her, as my mother raised her face to the water-stained ceiling.

That night, the coldest in 1956, was the first time I heard the sound two bodies make pressed together in bed. In the dark apartment, dried red flowers from the first of May lingered in a drinking glass.

Two

Things You Take With You

Berlin, 1958

I REMEMBER SITTING ON THE STAIRS TO OUR building in the communal courtyard, holding a small metal insignia. It's red and round. I like opening and closing my fingers around it, concealing it in my palm. A treasure, cool to the touch. I've had it since the night before and I can't stop looking at it, feeling it tug at something unfamiliar inside me. It was a button cover, or pin, from an old uniform. Hammer and sickle, diagonally crossed. It's similar but not quite the same as the Party symbol they display absolutely every-where. There are children playing close by, among the exposed tree roots, trying to start a fire with stones. But everything is too damp. Martina is crouched beside them, drawing in the dirt with a stick. As I turn the little pin toward the sun, three gold letters shine: PCE. *Partida Comunista Española*.

Papa had gone south two days before, for training near Potsdam, organized by the factory. He'll be back late, Mama told us when she picked us up from music lessons. I hate learning the *sol-fa*, Martina replied, walking a few steps ahead and nibbling on an apple. Papa never left Berlin on his own. At that point, we had only left as a family on one occasion, to visit some of our parents' friends in Leipzig. They also spoke Spanish and spent the whole weekend reminiscing about the old days in another city. It was a nice visit; we joked about everything, the rules, the food, the Soviets, the songs they taught us in school. It was Papa who said, that's enough, *familia*, we should be grateful to this republic.

We never saw them again.

The next summer, Mama enrolled me in a camp for workers' children organized by Papa's factory. The camp was in the Harz mountains, and I went on my own. It was the very first time I saw a steam engine, dragging its wagons through the peaks like a metal worm.

The days had grown longer: the afternoon sun shone through our single window, beating down on the living-room table. Martina and I spread out our homework and sat across from each other. When we finished, Mama looked over our notebooks and said, you girls can go play for a bit. She spent a lot of time on our maths work; they even do division differently, she said. Then she went to bring the dry laundry down from the rooftop.

Martina wanted to play hide-and-seek. I took a sock and covered my eyes. One, two, three, up to ten. Martina? Are you in here? No! Martina shouted from the bathroom. We played a few times. This is the last time, I want to read, I said. Come on: one, two, three, four, five, six, seven, eight, nine, ten. Here I come. Where are you? But Martina didn't answer. Say something! Give me a hint. I searched for Martina all through the apartment, but she was nowhere to be found. There was only one place I hadn't looked: under our parents' bed. I pulled the sock from my eyes and felt around under the bed frame with my foot. Are you under there? I didn't feel anything. I crouched low. Martina's head peeked out from behind a set of suitcases. I reached under the bed and pulled on my sister's arm, dragging the suitcases out with her. We looked at each other, Martina's lips white as I tugged on one of the handles. Pressed cardboard, held together with two dusty string cords. I undid the knots.

I heard a basket of clothes drop to the floor with a sharp smack behind me and I let go of the photos I was holding. Mama entered the room slowly, as if her body weighed a tonne. She leaned against the wall beside me and slid to the floor, her small bones seeming to have lost their structure. She began to undo my braid, burying her fingers deep in my hair, never taking her eyes off the suitcase. Without a word, she picked up the papers we had taken from the suitcase, the yellowed documents, and then sent my sister to the living room to colour. But Martina went no further than the doorway, where she stopped, still clutching a photograph. Time passed. I don't know how much. Whenever Mama's eyes met ours, they were unfocused. At some point our father came home, whistling to us from the front door: girls, I'm back. No one responded, so he came into the bedroom. He saw the suitcases, our mother sitting on the floor. He began to shout, pacing the apartment. He said the things one says to children. And he said them in Spanish. The only thing we've ever asked of you, the only thing your mother and I have ever asked, he repeated again and again, until I heard the quick step of his boots on the stairs. The afternoon was over.

There's a lot you won't understand. You still don't really know about the war.

I do know, Mama. Some things. I do.

Not this war. Our war.

Mama's fingers barely traced the images she held in her hand, as if she were afraid she could erase them.

You have an aunt. In Madrid. My sister, Carola. That's her there, and this is me. And an uncle, your father's brother. His name is Gabriel and he has two children, Moses and Manuel, like your father. They're in Moscow. This is him, here.

Do you write to your sister?

Rarely.

And are you sad you're not with her?

Very.

Why did you have to leave?

Mama didn't answer.

This is what we took with us when we left, Papa said when he returned and found us there, hugging our mother. Mama had finally stopped crying, but my nose was sore and red from blowing it. I cried like I hadn't cried since the time when I was little and went down to the courtyard by myself, without permission, looking for Thomas and Alexandra, and Mama came down with her arms crossed and forced me to come out from behind the trees, spanked me lightly on the bottom and dragged me back upstairs quickly, stumbling. It's all we had left, Mama said. This is it. She pushed her way through the bedroom door and stood in the front of the window, thinking about the war for a long time. Mama was never angry. She cried with her own sort of sadness. Red, silent. No one said another word about it until the next day.

I couldn't sleep that night. I tried to memorize the faces I had seen. Aunt Carola was prettier than Mama, or younger, I don't know which. But they both smiled as they sat in wicker chairs outside, embroidering a large piece of fabric. And held tight in my hand, a talisman. The little red pin I'd decided not put back in its place in that strange suitcase, the one I'd seen fastened on the coat our father was wearing in one of the pictures. Scrawled on the back of the photo: *With my brother, Gabriel, Madrid 1937.*

Three

The Blood of Sardines

Berlin, 1961

THE LAST TIME I CROSSED THE CITY – BOTH
sides of it, that is – Mama had sent me for food. Go
now, before it gets dark. She wrote an address on a
piece of paper. A Spanish last name. Go, and tell him
to give you what's ours. Don't open what he gives
you – put it in with the fish, inside the paper. But
don't open it. Remember everything I say, Katia. We
had fish every few months and, to get it, you had to
go to the West.

I left the apartment and went straight to wait in
line for our weekly egg ration at the produce stand on

the Bersarinstraße. It would have made more sense to collect them on my way back, but I was lucky – the wait was only half an hour. I didn't feel like speaking to anyone. I had a long walk ahead of me. Why me, Mama? Who else should I ask, Katia? Your little sister? Or maybe I should go myself? Who would work in my place? You? And who . . . ? I held out the ration card so the shopkeeper could count the members of our family: a picture of two girls with long braids, dressed alike, and a couple, still young – he smiled, she did not – and the unmistakable red stamp below our faces: exiles. He gave me four small, cold eggs. With gloved fingers, I picked off a few feathers and bits of filth. I stared at one of the shells, now clean: it would be so easy to crush, the egg white would drip from my hand, clear and viscous, down to the ground. I stood still and tightened my hand around the egg very carefully until a woman, waiting her turn, tapped my elbow. I took the scarf from my hair and made a little cloth nest, cradling the eggs inside it.

I crossed the skeleton of the Bersarinplatz with its mountains of rubble. The intersections, at least, had been cleared. Once a week, we secondary school students worked cleaning the streets, students and the *Trümmerfrauen*, the war widows who scoured Germany's ruins, amassing bricks to build the country anew. The streets were clean but rocks still slept in giant piles, the remains of a city my family hadn't known, a city before our time there. Our work consisted of chipping cement off the bricks. With our miniature pick axes, we stripped the remnants of Nazi Germany in service of the Government.

It took me more than a half an hour to walk to the river Spree. I recalled the geography lessons I had memorized and crossed the river over Oberbaumbrücke, leaving the black water behind me. I'd made this trip several times before, with Mama. And though we hadn't been pursued, we had walked quickly away from the border, Mama pulling me by the hand, hers in mine, gripping me tightly, as if she feared I could stumble at any moment. She had told the soldier we were visiting family. I took the same route now and entered the Kreuzberg market. Don't stop, Mama had said, don't dilly-dally looking at the stalls, but that day I stood very still in front of a fruit seller: I suddenly imagined that I could taste orange on my tongue, liquid and sweet. I found the fish stall and ordered four sardines, as I'd been told. The fishmonger laid the four fish in a few sheets of Western newspaper. Could you … ? I said. Ah, yes. The man looked at me over the fish and understood that returning to our Berlin with Western newspaper would only bring me trouble. He took out some plain brown paper and wrapped them up. That won't hold, I thought.

I carried the address in my pocket. In cursive, with sloping and widely spaced letters, Mama had written 'Requena'. I crossed several streets and found the building. I could see the black-and-white checkerboard floor in the entryway through a glass pane on the big door. I rang the bell and they opened without a word. I climbed more than a hundred stairs, the bag of sardines hanging from my arm. The door to the apartment was open. Hello? This way – are you Isabel's daughter? Yes, Katia. Well then, Katia, this is for you. Careful crossing.

Requena – or whatever he was really called – had small eyes and brillantined hair. He handed me an envelope. An address I didn't recognize, somewhere in West Berlin. Nothing on the back. No return address. All right? Did you want something else? No, sir. I left and began the walk back home. A large crowd had gathered on the Köpernicker Straße and were shouting at a few soldiers dragging wire fencing across the asphalt. I stood with them, but couldn't see much of what was happening. What's that smell? A man turned to me. The fish had soaked through the brown paper and liquid was accumulating in the bottom of the bag. I took off running. When I reached the checkpoint, one of our policemen stopped me: what do you have in there? Nothing. It's dripping blood, take it out. Between his feet and mine, four red drops.

The guard took the bag and unwrapped the paper. Four cadavers, open eyes bulging, the sun shining low over the Spree. What's this? Fish, I said. Please, I thought, please, keep them but don't find the envelope. The policeman stuck his hand in again and tugged on the scarf, unravelling the little nest. The four eggs fell to the ground. Don't cross for this again, he said. No, sir, thank you. I somehow managed to run until I was well past Warschauer Straße. Then I sat down, between the trees, and confirmed that the letter was still hidden with the sardines. It was wet and pulpy, soaked with blood. I wiped the envelope on my socks and blew, dry, dry, come on, dry.

I didn't think of the eggs until I reached home three hours after I'd left. Mama opened the door, gave me a kiss, and stuck out her hand. She didn't remember them either.

It's from your aunt. I've been waiting for a month.

Who's Requena, Mama?

He receives letters for us, in the West. They would never arrive if he didn't take them, coming from Spain.

Because they're Fascists?

Don't talk like that, *hija*. And not a word of this, not to anyone.

A short time later, Papa came home with Martina. Mama kissed him on the mouth. She was smiling, at last. News? he asked. Come, she said. And they shut themselves in their room. When he came out, Papa lit a cigarette, his figure silhouetted against the window as Mama prepared the sardines. She pressed on their heads and pulled toward the tail, ripping out the guts just as she'd done many times before. And then the shiny scales crackling over the heat, the heavy odour filling the room. No one opened the windows.

A few days after Mama received the news of her nephew's birth, and just a few streets from our building, the wall went up. To stop our country being bled dry, the radio announced. The fishmonger, the bright red entrails spilled on ice, the stall with its stacks of fruit, and the man who took letters for our family, were all left on what would then be known as 'the other side'.

Many years later, I understood the scale of the human machinery that had been required for those letters to reach us, just how many cogs had to turn,

They built the Stalinallee with bricks salvaged by school children and widows, erected its towering statue overnight. And all the rest.

only stopped once to fill the tank and enter the shop, returning with a bottle of Vita Cola. You girls share it, he said. He got back in the car and started to drive. The smell of eucalyptus cooling cream turned my stomach.

I spent the rest of the trip home craning to watch myself in the rear-view mirror, admiring my colour from our days at the beach, my hair marbled with a few blonde highlights. Martina noticed and imitated me, tossing her hair, closing her eyes and pursing her lips. That was the first summer that we didn't wear the same style of bathing suit. She had inherited the red-and-white one piece I had worn to the lake the year before. For this trip, Mama bought me a navy-blue striped suit with uncomfortable lining at the chest.

It was dusk when we reached Berlin. The city seemed more ramshackle than ever. Papa parked in front of the courtyard gate and took the suitcase out of the trunk. Between the four of us, we wiped the car down with damp rags, scraping off dead insects. Wait for me here, I'll bring the car back to Günter. Papa's friend from the factory who lived one street over had lent us a white Trabant for the trip. I can't believe he actually lent us his car, my mother said. You see, Isabel? People here are generous with their belongings. The State maintained a ten-year waiting list to buy a car. When people got one at last, they took care of it like another member of the family.

Five minutes passed and Papa was back. He grabbed the suitcase and we crossed the courtyard and began to follow him up the stairs. But Papa stopped. He raised his hand, holding us back. We stood motionless on the landing. Martina had to pee, bouncing on her toes like a spring.

What's wrong, Manuel?

Nothing, wait here.

Mama put her arms around our shoulders and pulled us close. We heard the key turn in the lock, the door as it closed. A long moment passed and a man we'd never seen before came down the stairs quickly from our apartment. A minute later, another man. The second man put his hand on Martina's head, ruffling her hair brusquely. Papa looked down into the stairwell and told us to come up.

An administrative issue. Something I'll have to take care of tomorrow. Don't worry.

It's because we went away, Mama said.

No, love, no.

When we opened the door to the apartment, everything was just as we'd left it.

Papa left early the next morning. It was Saturday. Mama washed all the clothes we'd brought on the trip and was back and forth to the roof, hanging it up to dry. We ate lunch, the three of us, and Martina fell asleep next to Mama on the couch. Mama did some calculations in a notebook in silence. I asked for permission to go down to the courtyard. Go ahead, but come up now and then, so I know you're okay, she warned. Alexandra was spending a few days at a camp for the children and relatives of workers at her father's factory. I hadn't seen her since the school year ended. I sat on the stone bench, and, after a minute, Thomas appeared.

I watched him come bounding down the fire escape, skipping the last few steps of each section. The sound of his shoes on the stairs, a leap, and *whap*! Two feet on the landing. Thomas had been my first friend. We went to school together and our mothers took turns collecting us at the end of the day. His sister, Alexandra, was a year younger. They were both very blond, white-blond, especially Thomas. He had a long fringe he was constantly blowing upward.

How was the beach?

Good.

You're tanned.

A little.

And blonder. You look almost German, he joked.

I shook my head and gave him a forced smile. The skin on my legs, still warm from the sun, was covered in goosebumps from contact with the cool, shaded stone.

I have a girlfriend, he said.

Oh, yeah? And what fool wants to be your girlfriend?

I'm not going to tell you.

She probably doesn't exist.

She does so exist. Her name is Lisselotte.

What kind of name is that? And where is she? I don't see her, I said, squinting, pretending to look between the trees.

We both went quiet. I felt like I'd said something stupid. Thomas jumped up on the bench.

They caught a woman this weekend, near here.

What?

She was trying to escape to the other side. Want me to show you where?

I can't go anywhere, I said. And besides, how do you know?

Because my father was on his way home from work when it happened. Come on, let's go, what's the big deal? We'll go and come right back. You can borrow Alexandra's bike.

I followed Thomas for close to twenty minutes. We stopped one block from the wall. Thomas told me the woman had jumped through yards and gardens, looking for a ladder or a shed to use to climb over the wall. She just kept climbing over everything in her way. If you got close enough, you could see the blood, dried now, where she had held on to the fence, Thomas said. She had crawled in the trenches as though she believed she were invisible, invisible under that stark, artificial light that illuminated everything and turned night into day. Just when she was almost across the death strip, she found herself face-to-face with a German Shepherd dog. It attacked. At first, it might have mistaken her for another dog, because it started to sniff her. But the woman had stood up and started to run, and the dog sank its teeth into her trousers. The woman was shot in the leg. She surrendered.

There's no way you can know all that. They never talk about that stuff.

That's what the neighbours told my father.

I was quiet for a moment, deep in thought, then I picked up the bike and started home as fast as I could. I thought about my father and the men who had been waiting for him. Katia! Hey! What's wrong? Thomas shouted, standing to pedal. Are you scared or something? Wait for me. He caught up with me quickly and cut off my path. I was upset. We sat down, our backs against a building. Thomas held me.

And your girlfriend?

Back home, I sprinted upstairs. Mama didn't even give me time to open the door. She slapped me right there in the doorway, where have you been, and started to cry, her agony exploding in my face. I locked myself in the bathroom for over an hour. The red mark on my cheek left by Mama's fingers faded slowly, some kind of bleak consolation. But there was another kind of commotion gaining strength within my body, parts that pulsed: the sudden taste of Thomas's hot tongue in my mouth. Daring. Rough. Submerged.

Papa didn't come back until the next morning. He went straight to his room and slept until dinner. For two whole days, he didn't speak. My striped bathing suit sat on top of the pile of clothes in the laundry basket, idle after our days away, the thrill of the Baltic waves.

Nothing had happened there, in the end.

Five

Fighting Boy

Berlin, 1968

DO YOU EVER THINK ABOUT WHAT IT MEANS to be here for ever?

No. I don't. What language do you dream in, Katia?

What do you mean, what language do I dream in?

We were on the banks of the Spree. With cold lips, I spoke into the wool of Thomas's sweater. A few pale strands of his hair stuck to my mouth.

A few hours earlier, we had met at Mischa's apartment on the Kiefholzstraße. The longest section of the avenue was in West Berlin; the remainder fell on our side. It was one of the grimmest streets of all, grey and barely even finished in the East, full of noise and bustle on the other side. It was the least-watched and southern-most crossing in the city. There, the border narrowed. West Berliners had built terraces that rose higher than the wall so they could look over and watch. They brought students there on field trips. The teacher said: what you see there is the Communists' Berlin, and they jotted notes in their notebooks, pointed their fingers at us. When we were about to enter Mischa's building, a couple of kids in bright neon jackets threw a few chocolates down to us. Thomas bent to pick them up.

Hey, we're not supposed to feed the animals, one said.

Oh, come on. The boy's not so bad, said a girl. He could be cute.

The others laughed.

I grabbed Thomas's hand and we went inside.

What's wrong with how I look, he said, inspecting his reflection in the foyer mirror.

Steam from boiling peas clogged the stairwell.

Mischa's parents had gone to visit friends in

Thüringen, so the place was empty and we'd made plans to meet some of our companions from the Freie Deutsche Jugend.* Three years earlier, Mischa had enlisted in the People's Army and was now about to leave to study in Moscow. Jutta, his girl-friend, had brought a Rolling Stones record her uncle Heinz had snuck through. Every month, Heinz managed to pass a few things along to the family. Once, Jutta gave me a pair of sheer nylon stock-ings, knee-high. I put them on and went out with Thomas on a walk. Show them to me, he said. I lifted my skirt, just to where the lace trim began. When Mama found them, she threw them out. Your father better not see these.

We played the Stones album quietly, several times in a row. Mischa wrote down the lyrics by ear on a piece of paper. That day at our friend's makeshift fare-well party, we danced – absurdly – to the muted music as if we were at a sold-out stadium show. Jutta's body was in constant motion, dancing off by herself, or in front of Mischa and Thomas. She was pretty, I guess:

---

* Free German Youth

the dark eyes, ginger hair cut short, big breasts and narrow hips. She wore threadbare jeans and a light-coloured shirt that showed her belly button when she lifted her arms. I felt small and clumsy next to her, a woman in slow motion.

Jutta started to tell us how she'd heard that, for the anniversary of the GDR, the Stones had been going to play on the roof of the Springer publishing building so that we'd be able to see them here in East Berlin, too. My sister went to the wall with a few of her friends, she said. Nothing. My uncle Heinz told us that the rumour was everywhere and that it had turned out to be a prank, started by a Western editor. People believed it because the Beatles had played on a roof in London a few months before. I heard this song is banned on a lot of stations in the United States. For being subversive.

Well, I think it could be a Party song. It sounds anti-Capitalist to me. Turn it up, Mischa.

As he spoke, Thomas jumped up on the couch, shaking his head and playing air guitar. Time to fight in the street.

Keep your voice down, Thomas, I said. On the

other end of the couch, Jutta had already climbed on to Mischa's lap. Let's go.

Just then, Jutta stuck her hand in her pocket and pulled out a wadded-up ball of newsprint. Inside were sweet potato seeds. Thomas and Mischa had wanted to try them for a while. Once, they said, a guy had offered them a handful of twenty or thirty. You washed them down with beer and they made you hallucinate and really feel like talking. I put on my coat. No, thanks, I said. Let's go.

We left Mischa's and walked in silence. We crossed Plänterwald. A Western car drove up slowly beside us. Food! Thomas shouted at them, stretching out his hand, we need food! What are you doing, Thomas? The men stopped and rolled down the window, one of them pointed a camera at us. Imbeciles, Thomas said.

We walked for a long time. We didn't take the route that followed the river. We crossed Treptow. The meadow was damp and smelled of rotting vegetation. Hardly any people were in the park. In the distance, blue smoke threatened from the chemical

39

plants. Thomas grabbed my hand and pressed me against the railing on the Abteilbrücke. He was very close. Our breath a challenge in the air between us. A policeman paused at the end of the bridge and Thomas pulled me away. We sat on a bench under a few trees, on a wooden dock on the Insel der Jugend. He drew circles in the Spree with the toe of his shoe while I asked him questions to which he responded with disinterest. Do you ever think about what it means to be here for ever?

Willow branches hung low, painting the dark bank green. Heavy evening air, a storm about to burst. Suddenly, brusquely, as if by reflex, he turned to me and unbuttoned my coat. I watched his fingers undo my cardigan, my shirt. I lay back on the dock. He pulled apart the fabric and exposed my old sports bra, the worn pink trim. I bent my knees. The chill of his fingers, digging in all over. Thomas put my hand inside his trousers and covered it with his own. We could barely move our fingers.

Come on.

I can't, I said. I just can't.

You're Spanish, and it shows.

I'm not Spanish. But I'm not Jutta either.

He stood and zipped his trousers, his anger grinding the dry leaves underfoot. He lit a cigarette, his back to me. The wind ruffled his blond hair. A passing pleasure boat sliced the water in two, the air in two. I'm sick of this, he said, his back still turned. I dream in German, I said, as Thomas walked away, leaving my words behind in a cloud of smoke, dispassionate words, not even spoken for him to hear. A line weakly cast, no intention to hook anything at all.

He didn't turn around.

I walked the banks of the Spree on my own until the Puschkinallee. Its ring of steadfast birches flanking the stone Soviet soldier. I looked up. Raindrops began to fall on the statue, on the child he held and the spade he drove into a swastika.

I continued home by tram, a knot in my throat as well as a sense of relief. Like Thomas, I had also been aroused at a certain point that evening, a moment firmly fixed in my memory: the chaos in my joints, my knees, my nostrils flaring, eyes rolled back, hypnotised, so unlike their calm counterparts in photographs. Yes, I'd lain down in the muck with him, started to allow myself to be pulled under by the same ardent quicksand – desire – that Thomas so welcomed. But I couldn't let myself go, in the end, or didn't want to.

The tram made several stops. Each time the doors opened, a fresh chill penetrated my bones. A man, his eyes smudged with dark circles, boarded and sat down across from me. He wore a navy coat and glasses. Two hands holding a briefcase. The man sensed me watching him and looked up, the dark circles, the grey eyes. Our eyes briefly met. I faked a yawn to hide my tears and, when I couldn't contain them any longer, I pressed my head against the window and cried. I felt as if I was dying more than once on that tram ride. Each time, the Stones song came back to my head, to my lips. Nothing had substance.

I got off the tram and watched as it passed the crossing and grew distant. The line would continue its journey to the city centre, beyond our neighbourhood, beyond the stick of dynamite that had just exploded between Thomas and me.

I looked at my shoes, covered in mud and grass.

That night, I dreamt in my mother's tongue.

Six

The Anna Seghers Book

Berlin, 1969

*A fear that had nothing to do with a bad
conscience; it was a poor people's fear, a chicken's
fear under a hawk, a fear of being persecuted by the
State. An ancient fear that better defines to whom the
State belongs than any constitution or history book.*
Voices tangling, like pipe smoke in a beard. Miss, he
said. Miss. Papa's paperback open on my lap under
the table, and me, lost in the pages. My red corduroy
coat, folded beside me, the leather satchel filled with
books, papers, threads of tobacco. I came to attention and the professor was standing next to me, arms

I left class and meandered towards the Karl-Marx-Allee. That Berlin cold. Face the sun in the winter and you'll get sick, our mother used to say. I felt pretty that day and I walked with my head held high. For my eighteenth birthday, Mama had made me a woollen dress in green-and-white houndstooth. I told her what I wanted. A straight, button-up jacket with a Peter Pan collar. Skirt to the knee, straight as well. I'd modelled it for my family, who sat watching from the new sofa: *hija*, you look beautiful, you must think your old dad is an idiot, but I just realized that you've gone and grown up. I had cut my hair, too, doing away with my braid – to my mother's chagrin. A side-parted fringe now covered one eye.

I went into the Café Sibylle. It was the only place in the city where you could still get an espresso. In the rest of East Berlin, you could only find *Milchkaffee*, a blend of 51 per cent coffee and 49 per cent rye, chicory and beet. The price of coffee had risen sharply in recent years and our currency had collapsed, but it wasn't the time to snatch away another of the people's pleasures. I had only been inside the Sibylle once, back when it had been called Milchtrinkhalle. I had gone

with Mama when she met a Spanish friend for coffee.
They talked and laughed the whole afternoon, while I
flipped through books and scuffed my shoes together,
trying to dull the shine.

I sat at a table in the large front window and
stared out at the street, my mind elsewhere. The white
buildings shone in the morning sun. I opened *The
Seventh Cross* again. I hadn't bothered to mark the
page where I'd stopped and it took me a moment to
find the line I'd been reading. The story: seven prisoners escape from a concentration camp in Westhofen.
The repressive machine leaps into action in pursuit of
the escapees, promising to catch them within a week.
They order seven trees stripped of their branches and
a board nailed across the trunk in the shape of a cross.
We will hang them as we find them, the head of the
camp swears. We will execute them in front of all
the other prisoners. The book describes the capture –
'dead or alive' – of the first six. The remaining seventh
cross, empty, becomes a symbol. Without ceding an
inch to sentimentality, Seghers narrates the fugitive's
flight and all that befalls him, his struggle to survive,
his wait for word of the others. She knew that to

follow the movements of the last remaining fugitive – George – in his terror, would make the book almost unbearable to read. *We all felt how profoundly and how terribly outside forces can reach into a human being, to his innermost self. But we also sensed that in that innermost core there was something that was unassailable and inviolable.* I was reading that sentence when I realized that a young man was observing me from a few tables away. It was the second time that day someone had ripped me from my reading of Seghers. I didn't try the coffee.

brain, neurons, flash. A natural intricacy: the greater the emotion, the stronger the memory. Emotion is the filter and it is the tide. It's the revolution. The sharpness of a memory, its clarity, is tied to what we feel. Emotion, a simultaneous cascade of chemicals unleashed in the body, a surge both unstoppable and addictive. The end of critical thinking, of judgement. Dilated pupils. A small animal hiding from the State.

My important memories are gone from that time, those early days when I met him. I've lost them. I never reckoned on the possible consequences. Was it sin or survival? I don't know. What was Papa doing back then, how much had Martina grown, what was Mama's life like, as I prowled a clandestine Berlin? I would come home and act normally, but I was different. Changed. I bore an immense secret. I didn't talk when I came home. I got into bed and logged, mentally logged, everything that had happened. Outside: the streets, the shops, the wall, the university. Inside: supper cooking, Mama and Papa's greying hair, a visit from a friend. But I registered nothing of their unhappiness and fear. Nothing of the Party or the surveillance, the decrees, laws, the disappeared, the eyes. Straight hair, very tall, a bird-man. He wore an open jacket with two brown stripes on the shoulders. That's what I saw. He arched his brow and smiled. What? And I knew it, then: he wasn't from the East. He wasn't from the East. He was from the other side. A tourist, a student, but why had he followed me? Always a few paces behind, crossing the street, matching my pace, hanging back but not bothering to hide his pursuit. And now we were face-to-face, and it was where he came from that led me to speak, what could it have been if not that moment, a split-second, an impulse. What do you want? Nothing, he answered, just to meet you. Me? To meet me? Why? You seemed interesting, he said. I seemed interesting? The books were the only witness to those words, our first conversation. Papa on my shoulder, shush, Katia, don't speak to him, he's with the others, he isn't your people, what do you think he's after, a wife? Don't be stupid, child. But there was something else pushing at me, something lacking in foresight, obviously – a hurricane, a hazard, something strange that compelled me to answer him. A chain of unforeseen reactions. Unforeseen consequences. I smiled, but said that I had no interest in meeting him. And I turned away. My pulse, a drumbeat beneath my red coat, that red corduroy coat, under the houndstooth check dress and under my skin, an expanding heart, expanding lungs, reflex. We left the bookshop together without speaking, our arms brushing by chance as we walked, but there was not another word between us. I kept my eyes straight ahead, not a single glance except at his sneakers, blue, two white stripes on the side, worn from walking, but where? We stopped at a traffic light, heart and lungs, heart and lungs swelling, swelling inside, we stopped on the bridge, two silhouettes, we walked alongside no man's land until we reached the courtyard gate to my building, my elbows pressed tight to my sides, still not another word between us. There were the trees in the courtyard, twisted by winter, and, above, the light in the window where Mama and Papa would be, and Martina, perhaps. Stop here, I said. And he laughed, turned, and walked away. Before I went inside, I ran through the sequence, the series of events, the decision and its arbitrariness: Herr Tonnemacher, the university, the walk, the coffee left abandoned in the Sybille and everything that followed. That night, the night after I met him, I could hardly sleep. I tossed and turned, imagined possibilities: this won't end well, don't play. And I tried to forget our encounter, how ludicrous it had been.

And then Christmas time arrived, my last Christmas in Berlin. Papa brought home a turkey. It keeps coming undone, Mama said as she trussed it, the skin's too tight to sew. And it probably cost a fortune! I mashed walnuts and dried plums with a bit of cheese for stuffing that would later drip on the baking sheet. As always, we ate together. The four of us. The dry turkey, such a shame, Mama said, the burnt stuffing. Don't worry, *mujer*, at least we've got this, and Papa opened a bottle of beer and poured a little into each of our glasses. Then Happy New Year, and 1971 entered our lives just like that, full stop.

have seen your face. Papa went a few steps ahead and talked as we walked downstairs. That damp, grey stairwell, a pram parked in the hall, the smell of sauerkraut clinging to the walls. Do you remember the year the Three Kings left you the blue elf? The one with the little plastic face. Woolly hair. I don't think I've ever seen anything quite like it in my life. Horrible little thing. But you loved it. You cut its mouth with a knife so you could feed it and Mama and I couldn't figure out where the rotten smell was coming from. And there it was, inside the elf. Disgusting. Do you remember? Papa stopped in the courtyard and turned to pull my scarf up over my nose, like when I was a little girl. I blew a puff of air through the knitted wool and my breath disappeared between us. I'll never forget the feel of that scarf against my face. Mama had knitted two of them: a shorter one for Martina, and one for me. Hers was red with three green stripes at either end, and mine the reverse. The smell of livestock and laundry soap, traces of the warm stable and the shearer's hands, the thousand times Mama scrubbed it against soap and stone. Kings' day, *hija*! The only good Catholic holiday, isn't that right? Mama had through the dirty snow. Papa quickened his pace, tugging me, talking about things that didn't make much sense. We turned the corner. I didn't dare look back. At the bakery, nearly ten people were already waiting at the door. The snow started up again, it fell on Papa, who tried to ignore it, on Papa and me, it came down as if through an enormous sieve, damn snow, I said. Katia, enough already, okay? Papa exchanged one coupon for four white rolls. We went to Konsum and he bought the last bottle of Trinkfix cocoa and a tin of pineapple in syrup, which I hadn't noticed until we were home and he set it on the table in the living room. Are you crazy, Manuel? How could you spend that kind of money? Ah, let me be, *mujer*. Well, something rather strange happened while you were out, someone left a book at the door, *Canto general*, it says, Mama said, peering over her glasses. They rang, but when we opened the door nobody was there, just the book, and footsteps down the stairwell. I didn't even have time to look out of the window. That is strange, all right. A book in Spanish, eh? It must be from a friend, a *Reyes* present. Yes, must be, my father replied. I stared out of the window at the rectangle clear of snow his car had left on the street, and my father watched me. Here, maybe it's something you'd like. Papa handed me the Neruda book. I held it in both hands, and my fingers grazed the white cover, the red letters, 'América, 1950'. America. How long had he waited for me? I guess Katia doesn't want cocoa, Martina said. Wait, yes I do, I said, and sat down with the book on my lap. I opened my Kings' Day gift, a nickel pen engraved with my name. Martina opened hers, a box of tools. Mama chided my father for the expense: do you think we're made of money? That morning, everyone looked happy except me.

Nine

See You Never, Commander

Berlin, March 1971

THE CITY REMAINED WHITE, WHITE AND
silent until March. I failed Linguistics that winter.
Papa sat facing me, this is why we are here, killing
ourselves, do you think it's easy for anyone? You
shouldn't even be content to be second in class, and
now this? Now that. Everything was a disappointment. I was an absolute disappointment. I had spent
the last three months waiting, miles away in my head,
scared, no appetite, thrilled and depressed by turns,
terrified to see him again on some street corner, but
who was I terrified of, exactly? I didn't know. He

both was and was not there. Everything else lost meaning: my family, home, class, the city and its inhabitants. My father's reproaches a blip in time: standing before him, eyes fixed somewhere above his, yes, Papa, no, Papa, it's my fault, I know, I do. Everything you've been through. Everything I don't do. But inside of me, narcosis and mental block, the outside world moving as if in twilight, at half speed, and, at the same time, life was revealing itself to be something very simple, razor-sharp and fast. I had to hold on. I went to bed before everyone else. I sought that moment for myself. A few minutes to remember when we had stood face-to-face, the two of us. Every night his features contorted, a figure drawn in increasingly muddled lines.

And that book. Another reason to lie awake, imagining conversations that would never take place, feeling how I pulsed, below my waist and in my head too, in different places and different ways, something wild, rampant, almost impossible to return from. I had never really thought about how they lived, Westerners, their life so anathema to ours. To imagine him was to betray everyone, everything, around me. With every thought, I became the doomed daughter of the October Revolution.

They gave the Nobel to Neruda that year. And to Willy Brandt, the Chancellor of the Federal Republic of Germany, who was awarded the Peace Prize. Papa had shouted all through the apartment. What a farce! Mark my words, Isabel, this is the beginning of the end of everything we believe in. The end, Isabel. The end! Let's see what they do now. Those were the years of the Ostpolitik. We couldn't see over the wall, but the Westerners sold us their technology and we sold them raw materials for peanuts. Like two slow-moving galaxies, the two worlds began to approach one another. And like authoritarian parents, the two Germanies stretched the limits of our old, divided city. We lived in the middle. Surviving.

For solidarity against Imperialism, for peace and friendship! One summer evening, Papa tossed a pamphlet on the table in front of me. I stopped reading and office, she had already worked six hours in a textile mill. I saw her sleeping with her head on the reports more than once. She sent 60 per cent of her earnings back to the island. Julia told me stories about the revolution, the music of old Havana, the sand and the blue Caribbean waters, of Playa Girón. *Amiga*, I can't believe you don't know who Che is, I can't believe they haven't talked about him, what kind of Communists do you have here, anyway? And though we didn't have much free time, we managed to get out once in a while, go to a concert, drink beer sprawled on the banks of the Spree. She was a happy person. I loved how she spoke, the strange cadence of her voice, trimming her words so that everything sounded simple coming from her mouth. Julia always carried two photographs in her wallet: the blurred image of a group of young people holding up their fingers in a V and smiling, handkerchiefs knotted around their necks; and the other, a gorgeous woman in a bathing suit at the sea's edge. Two teenagers sat beside her, staring back at the camera. Her mother, with Julia and her brother. Julia was my first real friend, the way one's friendships at twenty can be. We told each

The first day of the weeklong festival, a photographer – a friend of our father's – came to take our picture in our Free German Youth uniforms. He photographed Martina next to the window first, outfitted in the blue shirt, red vest, and very short white skirt. I still don't understand this uniform, said Mama. I got dressed and posed beside my sister. Papa sighed with pride and wrapped his arm around our mother's waist. My mother gave me a look, imploring patience. I felt as I did when my father used to make me sing for his Spanish friends, the old Cossack songs he had taught me. Come on, *hija*, give us 'The Black Crow'. And he would plant me in front of him, two heavy hands on my shoulders, squeezing when I forgot the words or looked at the floor. Martina and I smiled, hers natural and mine forced, and off went the flash. Just then, I heard my name called from down in the courtyard. I looked out and there was Julia among the trees, waving up at me and accompanied by a group of other dark-haired kids laden with instruments. Papa opened the window. Come on, Katia! they shouted. Mama smiled at me and I went down. This is my brother, Alejandro. And this is his band, Julia told one of the boys. I had never seen anyone dance like that, cheek-to-cheek, in sync. Before I knew it, Julia's brother grabbed my hand and pulled me to my feet. I'll lead, he said. He put his hand on my waist and took my other hand in his. He stepped forward and back, slipping his leg between mine. Alejandro was studying to be an architect in Havana. He was nice, they all were. But something in that impromptu dance was disconcerting to me. Something just out of reach, something that left me stiff. And dancing with him, his slight body so close to mine, his hands, I became increasingly uncomfortable. Haven't you ever danced before? Not like this. I tried to let myself go. To stop thinking and take it in stride. But it was too difficult. It wasn't the music, it was that moment when he pulled me against him, when he said spin, and I went to spin on my own but he spun me instead. Alejandro's dark eyes looked into mine strangely. He was handsome, or maybe he wasn't, but he was different. I looked around for Julia and watched how she danced, I looked at those kids, not just the Cubans, all of them, the noise, the clash of music, the colours waving over the square, a space that was otherwise so grey, designed to leave you feeling insignificant. We looked like little animals someone had given all the tools required for a good time, look, see here, this is how the world's youth enjoys itself inside our borders, happy young people, happy young people forging our new Socialist world.

It happened, then. I don't know how many songs we'd danced through, but as I attempted to pass under Alejandro's arm, I saw him. He saw me too. He was standing very still, his arms pressed to his sides, big hands against his body, head tilted. His hair longer than the last time, a green shirt, jeans. Suddenly, everything seemed to crack. He turned and walked away in the opposite direction. I dropped Alejandro's hands and ran after him. Katia! *Chica*! Where are you going? What's wrong? I glanced back and saw Julia pulling at her brother, holding him back. I ran through the entire square, I couldn't believe it, I had lost him again, I collided with the crowd, a bad day to search for someone in Berlin. Breathless, I reached the tree-lined boulevard Unter der Linden and doubled over, hands on my knees. It's not meant to be, I thought. Never. But when I looked up, he was there in front of me, a spectre amidst the commotion, the merriment, the loudspeakers. He was very serious, but he was there.

We sat on the front steps of the museum and he held out a canteen filled with water. Do you want some? I didn't answer. I'm Johannes, he said. I remembered how Alejandro had tried to follow me, frustrated by our interrupted dance, stuck there with outstretched arms, hey, what's happening, I don't understand, and I started to laugh, anxious and absurd. Does my name amuse you? No, I said. And what's your name? The words stuck in my throat. It was what I had been waiting for, what I wanted, and yet I couldn't speak. That isn't quite true – I could have spoken, sure, but I knew that I shouldn't, though not the reason, was it me, or something else? Katia. Katia? Not Katja? No. You don't look like a Katia. And then he laughed. What did he mean, I didn't look like a Katia? What the hell was I supposed to look like? He stood and then crouched in front of me. He loosened the handkerchief around my neck. This uniform looks good on you. I asked him why he left on Kings' Day. What day? The day you brought me the book. Would you

Johannes and I took advantage of the excitement that gripped East Berlin in those days of the festival and walked the city like any other couple, holding each other, quiet at times, always looking behind us, aware of our surroundings. Scanning the people who strolled through the parades of musicians. There was something in the way he held my hand. So tight I knew he wasn't going to let go. And I remembered his breath on my face, closer and closer until his mouth was so near mine that, when we spoke, our lips collided, coming together and coming apart, and I tried to look down, to breathe through the tangle of nerves in my stomach. The mere memory of it was like someone had accessed an increasingly dormant part of my conscience, activating my guilt, *through my fault*, my father coming in from work, *through my fault*, my mother crying, a piece of paper in her hands, *through my most grievous fault*, forgetting Martina's parade. You'll come with me. This is what Johannes had murmured in my ear before he got into that car I already recognized, before he dropped me off several streets from home as I trembled, before he crossed the border and drove home under the same sky, where the same clammy light of the German summer would shine on both our faces, each on our own side.

I woke up the next morning and tried to gauge the household mood. Papa was scraping the last bits of Trinkfix from the container and tapping the spoon into his mug. Mama was mending a pair of short socks beside the window. Her glasses had slid down to the tip of her nose, and for the first time I noticed the lines round her eyes, little sunken threads. My parents were still young, and they were healthy, but I was suddenly aware I wouldn't always have them. Mama looked me over and continued with her work. Did you have a good time? Tell us about it, my father said. How was Martina? I replied, shifting the conversation to my sister. Oh, you should have seen your father fawning over her, it was so embarrassing, Manuel. The proud papa. Telling Fritz: my daughter, that's my daughter, my youngest, like a madman, Mama said as she drew a bead of blood from her pricked finger. Martina dragged herself out of bed, her hair a mess. Good morning. She pulled up a chair beside our father and rested her head on his shoulder. I poured myself a mug of coffee and gripped it in both hands, feeling how the enamelled tin warmed from bottom to top. An image flashed from the day before: during our walk in the Mitte, Johannes' fingers had teased the hair at the nape of my neck and, like an electric current, a shiver ran up my spine – it was as if the ends of my hair really had nerves – and seized my throat. My mouth opened. A feeling like I'd never known had parted my lips. And I was afraid that all of Berlin could surely sense that half-centimetre gap, spreading in slow motion. I put down the mug, which had started to burn, and touched my neck where his hand had been. Katia! What? Did you go deaf yesterday, what's the matter with you? What is it, Mama? I said, sit down and eat with your father and sister. I sat.

I didn't speak to Johannes again until after the summer. The city returned to normalcy, its wide avenues emptied, our Berlin was back under surveillance. I did manage to see him a few more times, however. Sometimes, we just walked along opposite sides the street. I was never able to predict which weekend he would reappear. On one of the last occasions, he gave me a photograph that I hid under my mattress and brought out every morning to take with me wherever I went.

In those days, Papa was spending more and more time away from home. One night, I had just switched off the light when Martina spoke: Could Papa be having an affair? That's crazy, I replied.

Ten

Out of Bounds

Berlin, Autumn 1971

THE LANGUAGE DEPARTMENT'S READING room became my favourite place in all Berlin. Papa was the one who first brought me there, when I was still deciding what to study. He had stood before the wide announcement board and examined the Romance Languages course schedule. Let's see what they have to say in Spanish, he said. We entered the classroom together, but I sat a few rows behind him. His beard had grown so long that it reached his forearms, crossed in front of him. And was the nape of his neck looking whiter all of a sudden? The blackboard that we were together. But he motioned with his chin after everything the professor said, raising his eyes and shaking his head, incredulous. The professor was trying to make himself understood with the wineskin and a few words. *Spanien, trinken, beber, vino*. When the class finished, he approached us and invited us to join him at a beer hall not far from our home. Papa accepted. The man told us he owned a bookshop in Lichtenberg. That it was so nice to speak Spanish. We all miss it, don't we? When the Nazis pulled out of Berlin, the Humboldt was suddenly bereft of professors, so they had to hire whoever they could, as you can see, he said, pointing to himself. But you sell books, you must like to read, Papa said. Me? Not at all, but one has to earn a living. Between teaching and the shop – which my family runs – we manage. If I only told you—. And I asked him to go on, yes, I nodded, tell us, but my father's eyes locked on my face. I opened mine wide back at him, trying to make sense of his expression. What? I said. The man laughed. Where should I start? How far back shall I go, *niña*? To when I was a *republicano* or when I hung Franco's portrait in the bookshop to throw off the Nazis? Papa stiffened and looked around, and I watched as he drained his glass. De Vega didn't give him a chance. *Hombre*, come on, I didn't even say anything. Papa was rigid. You think you can tell me anything about life? Survival, more like it. The man ordered another beer and Papa gave his account. And the guy laughed loudly, as if he was suddenly able to fit Papa and I like pieces into a puzzle that – at the time – hadn't yet begun to interest me. He observed us, hunched over his glass, laughing out loud. A droplet of beer stuck to his blondish moustache and I started to get the impression that he didn't want to be there either. You have to take things as they come, friend, one after another, he said. Papa grabbed my arm and pulled me out of my chair, I'm not your friend, he said, and we left, striding down the whole length of the Karl-Marx-Allee. Papa stopped and let go of my hand. He looked at me, inhaled, and glanced behind him. For a moment, I thought he would retrace our steps, go back to the professor and settle what had happened. But even as we turned down our street, I could hear the sound of De Vega's laughter, the way he shouted as we were leaving: you might have won in summer, when people were out the streets again, sitting in the squares, the world seemed to be both too flimsy and yet too intense and my enthusiasm flagged.

Pondering my listless state, I glanced up from my book. Johannes was sitting across the table from me. He put a finger to his lips. What are you doing here? I wanted to ask. But Johannes had taken a book down from the shelf and started to read. Soft light shone on his hair and across the contour of his eyes, almost transparent in the gloaming. He didn't take his eyes from his book, but I couldn't read another word. I turned the pages mechanically, my mind a whir, forcing myself to keep my head down. For an hour, everything but my roiling insides was frozen in place. It was six o'clock in the evening and dusk in Berlin by the time we left the reading room. Me, first, then him. Miss, he said, you forgot your jacket. I took it without meeting his eye. Thank you. I looked up as I left the lobby under the watch of Lenin and his outstretched arm. Marx. Engels. I exited through the university gate and stopped to wait in the centre of the square. Now what? It was always *now what?* with Johannes. I sensed him leave the library behind

know where she went while we were there. That had
been our agreement, if you ever need me, just come
to my place and knock. I was very familiar with that
room. When they let Joan Baez's record in, Julia and I
spent hours lying on our backs, listening and looking
up until we had memorized very single song and every
single water stain on the ceiling. Her apartment was
even smaller than ours and she shared it with two
other Cubans, Maite and José. A poster of Che had
been tacked up in the tiny, windowless kitchen containing nothing but three chairs and a table next to
the hob. The silhouette of a bearded man, black on
red, the paper creased as it travelled over many kilometres, *hasta la victoria siempre*.

I already know what you're going to say and it's not
possible, I told him. Johannes turned around and smiled.
He pulled me over and we sat on the bed. Johannes
lay down on his side, his head in his hand. But Katia,
there are ... I know that already, I cut him off. But it's
not that easy. I know someone who can get you out
of here, I'll give you the address, go and see him, he'll
know how, it's actually not that hard, really. You don't
have to worry about anything, not money, nothing. But

you can't say a word to anyone. Not even Julia. Not your family. Johannes looked at me, his back against the bedroom wall and his legs splayed across the bed. I'm sorry, I know it isn't easy. It's anything but easy. I've come and gone. I've made this trip. Yeah, I interrupted him, but you're from the other side. Johannes got up and stood with his back to me, looking out of the window. I could see his reflection in the glass. He was handsome, everything about him was young, but his face wrinkled in seriousness. His nose was large and his eyes were small, there was a scar at the right corner of his mouth, a neat profile. I didn't know what the rest of his body was like. I could see his back and his shoulders, not very broad, and the blue shirt, the State's blue, and the trousers below. A black cat sat on the outside ledge, hypnotized by its own reflection. Johannes banged on the window and the cat disappeared. I don't know you, I said. I don't know you either, he replied. He didn't turn around, but started to speak.

I live in Backnang, a town in the south. I have a little brother. Björn. He's sixteen. There's a wall and five hundred and ninety kilometres between you and me. When I come, I leave on Thursday, after my last class,

84

and it takes me roughly eleven hours. It's a designated transit route. Passing through the GDR is like crawling through a tunnel: I'm surrounded, I'm watched. I can't leave the road, all exits are blocked. And then, there's the border search. The checkpoints. And sometimes they won't let me in, Katia. I have to turn around and go back the way I just came. Exhausted. Dead on my feet. My parents' names are Manfred and Theresa. My father was in the war. With the Nazis. He came back dead – no, wounded – what I mean is, he had no life in him. He works for the regional Government. Once, I asked him to tell me about the war. No. No, he said. When he came back, my mother was still living in the same village where she was born, and they knew each other from before. They started to spend time together and they got married. We live in the house that belonged to my grandparents. We have some land with a few apple trees. In the summer, Björn and I pick apples and bring them to the co-op. In exchange, they give us the most delicious Apfelschorle you've ever had, if you've ever had it, that is. I finish my engineering degree this year and will probably start working in the factory. They fabricate steel pieces, perfect gears. I like that sort of thing. My friends live in the same town. We play football on Saturdays and then grill meat in a nearby field. We won the regional league title. Just the one time, but imagine how that felt. The very best in all of Rems-Murr-Kreis. We came here the next weekend – to Berlin – to celebrate. Do you remember? A few of my team mates were outside the café that day. I went in out of curiosity, I wanted to see what it was like. And I saw you. I'd never seen anyone like you. In what way? I don't know – there was something different. And I wanted it. You. I followed you to that bookshop ... I lost track of my teammates and it took me two days to get back to Backnang. I had a girlfriend back home. She was pretty. Is pretty. We went to Stuttgart one time and spent a night in a hotel and barely left the room the whole weekend. Elke plays the violin, her parents are friends with mine. But since that day, the day in the bookshop, I haven't seen her once. Because there's something, Katia, something that pulls me here time and time again. Do you know me? Do I know you? No. But when I start in the factory, I won't be able to come as often. I can't keep coming here. And that will be this summer.

Johannes went quiet and I didn't know what to say either. Why had he told me all of that? What was I supposed to say? That I would follow him, that I was that sort of audacious woman, even though I'd never even let a man put his hands on me? That, sure, in the East we were liberal and went around naked on the northern beaches but that I—. That at home, of course, but my family wasn't—. That only with Thomas, and that I told him *stop there*. Johannes started to speak again and, with every word, every one of his explanations, I imagined, I felt the pulse of temptation, a new life. And guilt, too.

Did you get the record?

What record? I said.

The Gilbert O'Sullivan record. I left it at your door the last time I was here.

What? I repeated. You left a record on my doorstep?

I went up and left it, after we said goodbye.

Are you crazy? Have you lost your mind? No, I didn't get it.

You gave me the Die Sputniks one the time before, so I thought you'd like to listen to something of mine.

I am strictly out of bounds.

Wow, so you speak English, too. I have to go, Johannes.

Hey, where are you going?

I don't know. Home. I have to get back. You left a record on my doorstep? I told you not to send anything.

I'm going with you.

Johannes walked me to the street before mine. He stopped me and stepped forward. He pressed against my body and undid the belt on my coat. He slipped his hand in at my waist, damp and warm from walking quickly, and brought his lips to my neck. And I knew in those languid, hazy minutes that I would leave for him. And that while some East Berliners risked their lives for an idea, for a life better – or worse – than ours, for the light on the other side of the wall, I would risk mine as well, but for an impulse, an impetuous instinct. He took his arm from my waist, grabbed my hand and gave me a slip of paper. It was small and lined, torn from a notebook and folded over. On it was written the end of everything I had ever known.

No Man's Land

Eleven

Poyejali

November 1971

I DIDN'T STEAL AWAY IN THE DEAD OF NIGHT.
I didn't have to creep past the neighbours. Like every
other morning, our apartment was empty. I wasn't
shaking as I packed a small bag with just four objects,
but I did tremble when I looked back at the living
room from the doorway. Memorizing that space. The
bodies that lived there, the sound of the door, keys
on the wooden table, a stew eternally simmering, my
family. Would I ever see any of it again? I left no note.
I left in silence, fighting to tamp down fear and doubt.
How worried would my mother be? Where would

they look for me? Seen from the outside, I was just Katia on her way to the university. But there were more layers than usual under my coat. And more commotion. Much more.

In my bag: the nickel pen; a Russian fur hat, I don't want this anymore, it makes me look old, Mama said; the Partido Comunista Española insignia pin I'd stolen from Papa; and an apple. *Poyejali*,* I thought. I was off like Yuri Gagarin on *Vostok I* and, like the Soviet cosmonaut, I didn't plan to find God on the other side.

I didn't take the tram at all. I walked for an hour and a half, like I'd been told to do. I crossed the whole city, our city. At some points, my route took me along the wall. Snow started falling. I pulled the fur hat down to my eyes, the black fibres tickling my eyelids. Then, there was the mud. And the path. The trees: trees and more trees. The sound of my steps as I gained ground, peeling my feet away from that dirt, my father's land, my father, the defender of all he'd planned for his daughters, our Berlin, hemmed

---

* 'Let's go!'

in. *Papá Estado*. Father State. Father, father. I walked that way, afraid, step by step towards all I had been told never to be. I wasn't wearing my Pioneer kerchief, but I felt it – I would always feel it – knotted at my neck, a stranglehold.

Then, there at the end, parked on a curve, a Trabant: engine running but lights dark, in spite of the snow. A man. It was time. I reached for the apple in my bag, took a bite, threw it. Like I was told. I kept walking. The car started to drive behind me, still at a distance. I heard it accelerate and smelled burning fuel. When it reached me, the man turned around, opened the door, and nodded. Get in. Wohin? I said, like they'd insisted. We didn't say another word for several hours. The smoke from the foundries on the outskirts of the city, lost behind us. A drier cold, harder to bear. We drove down a small road, black sand scattered and packed into the potholes. The man turned and gave me some papers. I'll speak for you. There was my picture, the one I had given Johannes a few months before, and the stamp of the State. The Government had approved my holiday in Czechoslovakia. A honeymoon.

Car's running slow, he said, suddenly.

But we drove on, toward the south of our Germany. Halfway to the border, the car started to slow on its own; the man was anxious. He glanced at me, gripped the steering wheel. We drove so slowly the snow grew thick on the windshield.

He turned and held out his hand. Your bag.

It's all I have.

We need it. Make do.

I gave him the bag and put the pen and pin in my pocket. I wore the hat, grateful for its warmth, traces of my mother's warmth. I took it off and held it to my face. Inhaled. Misgivings, then, but we'd gone too far to turn back. Can you turn around? That question could have changed our course, but I did not ask. The man pulled over on to the shoulder of the road. The car was on a slant, lopsided, and I slid against the frozen metal of the door. He used my bag to wipe the snow from the windshield. I could barely see out of the window. He lifted the bonnet. The sound of metal.

We'll go faster now, I hope. The ignition coils were wet. I wrapped them with your bag. Get up front with me.

of the match. The car filled with smoke, but neither one of us opened a window.

They ordered a man out of the car in front of us and pushed him against the side of the vehicle. Two more soldiers approached, guns raised. They opened the trunk, grabbing bags, throwing them far from the car. One guard gestured to another, who came back with a saw a moment later. We couldn't see at first, but then: a woman, dragged out by the arms. Face down on the ground, hands behind her head. Shouts. A soldier dragged her to the kerb by her legs as she twisted, writhed. No, I said. The man motioned for me to stay calm, this was good luck, they had their daily catch. They detained the driver too. The couple walked ahead of the rifles, hands on their heads, and entered the patrol station, a series of white barracks. That was all we could see. One of the soldiers got in the car and moved it from the middle of the road. Another waved us forward. I couldn't control the quiver of my jaw. The cold, the fear. Under my trousers and stockings, my knees went weak. In a theatrical show of intimacy, my companion put his hand on my leg and unrolled the window. The soldier opened the door and asked us to step out: it was time.

We exited the car. The soldier motioned us over. The man took my hand and passed the soldier his papers. His hand was damp, and I squeezed it tightly. The skin of strangers, risking everything at some godforsaken point on a map. The guard asked for my documents. A few soldiers approached, but none raised his weapon. I missed the warmth of the car and would have gladly accepted a cigarette then. The soldier took our papers to the guard post. Through the window blurred with condensation, we saw him make a phone call. Snowflakes landed on my face, above my lip. The man's shoulders were white. When the soldier returned, he handed us our papers and nodded to the others. We could pass.

We returned to the car and I realized that I could feel my heart beneath my layers of clothing. The man started the engine and very slowly we left the border behind. Goodbye Germany, he said, with a glance in the rear-view mirror. He put a large hand on mine, and this time it was he who squeezed. That was it, girl. It was unexpectedly easy. We smiled. Only then did I study his face. He was young, his features hidden behind a beard. Green eyes, ringed in another, darker colour. Eyes that were used to smiling.

After a few minutes, the stiffness that had pinned me to my seat started to thaw, and little by little, my body began working again. Dry eyeballs moistened and my muscles relaxed. How long had it been since I had gone to the bathroom?

I looked back and there was my country, evermore distant. We were in Czechoslovakia. The snow on my lip melted and dripped into my mouth.

It tastes the same everywhere.

Twelve

A Night in Hřensko

THE MAN STOPPED THE CAR. THE SUN HAD already set. It had been dark for a while. We didn't know what time it was.

Grab your bag, he said. Then he remembered the coils, and apologized. He didn't smile.

He took a travel bag from the trunk and locked the car.

I put on my hat and stuck my hands in pockets, toying with my only possessions to make sure I still had them. The village curled along a river. I stood at the edge. The water flowed calmly down a canal. The banks were green with moss. The dampness was so thick I could barely breathe.

This is where the Kamenice and the Elbe meet, he told me. This water runs from the sea in the north, on the other side. You are in the lowest point in all of Bohemia.

We walked down a stone-paved street. The snow had just stopped. The checkpoint was hardly an hour behind us, but all the while we had been following the same narrow, descending road. The buzzing in my ears removed me from the distance we had travelled, as if it were a movie in which I no longer had a part. A huge rock hung in suspension over the tiny village. There was something different, yet disappointing, in all of it. I don't know what I had expected to find. The man opened the door to a rooming house and gestured for me to step inside. He spoke with a woman in Czech, handed her an envelope, and showed her our papers. From their tone, I sensed a certain camaraderie between them. The woman gave me a once-over, not bothering with even the hint of a smile. We followed her up a staircase and she opened the door to one of the rooms.

Dekuji.

The woman didn't reply and left us alone.

They would have already noticed I was gone. Mama would be terrified. My father would rest his head on his fist against window. I tried not to think about them. But old conversations came to me, Katia, help your sister, and came, Katia, *hija*, give me a kiss, and kept coming, Katia, we expect you to—. I lay down on the bed with my coat on. I thought about what it meant, the word 'never'. And what I had chosen to pursue: Johannes. What I had done. I looked towards the window, and the darkness was the threat of all the nights that were still to come. All the nights and all the days. New air in another country. What have you done, Katia. What unwitting animal instinct had I allowed to pummel me, within my body and without it all at once, toss my whole life over a cliff's edge, shove each member of my family from the precipice and watch them fall one by one, *adiós*, gone, left behind for ever. Katia, daughter, sister, plotting her future in her own home, in her parents' home, in her own country. And I cried. Because I knew that when I opened my eyes the next morning, our foggy apartment window, my mother's constant activity, the warm smell of Martina under the blankets, asleep no matter what, a moment sitting with my father and listening to him breathe, my head on his chest, up, down, both of us breathing together, none of that was coming back. And like a frost, unexpected, creeping, something cold and white began to harden over those images. I did what I could to freeze my family inside. The man woke and said something like, it's okay, it'll all be different tomorrow. And, shifting under the covers, went back to sleep. One of his legs touched mine. I pulled away and lay on the edge of the bed. I couldn't fall asleep and I tried to think only of Johannes, about everything he meant, his trees ripening with apples under another sun, a house in another south, and his composure when he stood before me that first day, free of qualms and excuses. I didn't move until the next morning.

Before dawn, the man went out into the hall. He didn't turn on a single light. I heard him rinse his mouth with water in the shared bathroom. When he came back, he smelled of the same lotion my father used.

We have to go. Hurry.

I got out of bed and felt the weight of my eyelids.

I'm ready.

The man took my hand and pulled me down the dark hallway.

Steps, he said, twelve.

We crossed the foyer bathed in shadow and were off.

By the time the sun had risen, we had been in the car for almost an hour. We drove the whole day. I memorized the names of the first towns we passed. Even today, I could still trace our route. We stopped in Dêcín and got out to have coffee and bread at a roadside café. I hadn't eaten since sometime the day before.

Do you want another roll? No, I told him, I don't have any money. I've got your money, don't worry. Want another?

We asked for a few more rolls and this time they brought them with thick butter.

The man didn't attempt conversation. He simply drank his second mug of coffee and glanced around us occasionally. He didn't look afraid.

Once back in the car, my belly full, I drifted into a

strange sleep. My head felt as if I had been drinking. When the man slowed to pass a village or stop for petrol, I would open my eyes. One time, he was outside the car, chatting with a couple of soldiers. I wasn't worried. I'd released my fear and was waiting for what was going to happen to happen. I was tired. The man smoked with the soldiers. They spoke in Czech, laughed a little. I fell back to sleep.

We drove through Czechoslovakia. We were skirting Prague when the man told me he had a wife and son in Berlin. I had a father and a mother and a sister. The man didn't say anything else. There were no more questions. I didn't know where we were. And I didn't know where we were going.

Thirteen

The Trace a Body Leaves in Air

THE DOGS WERE THE LAST THING I HEARD before I crossed the river. I knew in that moment that it's not death we fear; what is truly terrifying is ceasing to live.

Things happened very quickly, but they're seared in my memory. The man, who was usually so silent, pulled to the side of the road and turned to face me. He gripped my shoulders with both hands: it's ten kilometres to the border. The next time I stop, you will open the door, get out, and walk. You will walk calmly and you will not look back. You will not say goodbye. Ahead of you, past the ferns bordering the path, there will be a forest of tall pines. You will walk in a straight line between them, as if they were arranged in order. Imagine a straight line between the tree trunks and follow it. Someone will take your hand and lead you. I've never made that part of the trip. My work ends here. Listen to me: if something happens, if whoever it is lets go of your hand, run through the forest as fast as you can. The border follows the river. If you don't know where you are, get in the water. Don't stop moving. Do you hear me, Katia? Never stop moving. The man spoke my name and I felt a deep anguish. The other side of the river was Austria.

I said goodbye then to the man. And I thanked him. Absurd words of thanks for someone paid to do something illegal. The man smiled. We looked at each other like two prisoners, as if one of us was condemned to die. We would never see each other again. The question hung in the air between us: is it worth it?

That's how it happened. I opened the door and passed through the first of the ferns, rough dampness scratching at my coat. A gloved hand caught mine and tugged. The hand of a young woman. I could make out the blonde braid hanging down her back. We ran. And then I heard the sounds of the border. Breaking glass. The girl pulled my hand and said: contraband. Bad. We heard the dogs. The forest was more unsettled. But we kept running. When we sensed the dogs were close, she let go of my hand and stopped in her tracks. I looked back. She had already started walking very slowly in the opposite direction. I kept running. I ran like I had never run before, with no idea when I would stop. Or where. Over the crunching of my boots, a siren wailed.

I never knew if it was me they were after, or the contraband carriers. But I made it to the river. I waded in and ran as best I could through the muck. I didn't look back. When I could no longer touch the bottom, I started swimming, weighed down by my coat, by water-swollen wool. But I didn't take it off, I had already lost too much. I did let go of my mother's Russian hat. I swam until my hands touched the soil of the bank. I grabbed on to the branches and pulled myself from the water.

I sat on the other side of the river's edge, the barking of the patrol dogs echoing in my ears. The black water still swirled where I had cut through the current. The moonlight reflected on the surface. I got to my feet and, where my body had been, there was nothing but trampled grass. I've crossed, I thought. On the other side of the river, the silhouettes of two soldiers and two dogs. Once the animals had settled and started sniffing the ground, one of the men raised his arm in a gesture of farewell. I lifted my sodden hand in return. *Auf wiedersehen.*

I found a road and reached the meeting point on foot, soaked, deathly cold, exhausted. I entered the walls of the old city through a gate adorned with a welcome sign. No soldier, no pointed gun. No one on watch. Nobody. Flowers hung from every window, faded blue under the night's dim light. I had lost the heel of one of my boots and I thumped along the cobblestones: one step, yes, one step, no. I sat on the ground beneath one of the porticos in the town square. I fell asleep. When the sun rose, I had a fever, my clothes were still wet, I was shaking, and there was Johannes and the deafening silence of all the things I no longer carried.

Fourteen

Not the Flag, Not Anymore

PAPA LEFT SPAIN IN 1938. MAMA, IN 1946.

They married in the midst of war. Just in case. *Abuelo*, my mother's father, strung a cord across the livestock shed from one end to the other, and the women tied up colourful pieces of cloth that hung down, grazing the heads of the guests below. But they didn't hang the flag. Not anymore. That's what Mama said. Not the flag, not anymore. Just in case. There was no wedding banquet. They drank the last cask of wine. The good wine, *Abuelo* told anyone who would listen. My eldest daughter is getting married and the dregs on the bottom of that clay jar are as old as she is. *Abuelo* had refilled that small barrel every fall, and the wine turned to brandy. One sip of that and you would dance all night, especially on an empty stomach. But they didn't dance either. Just my parents, who held each other and moved together. That wasn't dancing, Mama said. No music, so they wouldn't draw attention. After that night, my grandfather never refilled the barrel again. He died of exposure. Mama said that's what *Abuela* told everyone. He died on this day, on what – many years later – would be your birthday. 21 February. He went into the brush to cut cork to plug up the holes in the walls and he came back drenched. When *Abuela* removed his socks, chilblained skin peeled off with them.

Your father was just as silly back in those days, Mama continued. I'll never forget one time, during the village fair: Papa had bought a liberty cap at one of the stalls in the plaza. We were just sweethearts then and he was goofing around when people around us started running. He brought me to my parents' house and ran off. When he came to say goodbye later, he wasn't the same. They'd killed a man in front of the priest's house. I never knew what your father saw or didn't see, but that very night he left for the mountains, as a volunteer. He didn't come back until the summer of '37. He stayed in the village for three days. We got married on the third. His beard was down to his chest and he'd been eaten alive by bedbugs. He had lost the shoes my father had given him – my father had given him his only shoes – and he was wearing pieces of rubber strapped on with laces. Your grandmother almost fainted when she saw him coming down from the hills. He was skinny. Can you girls imagine your father, skinny? You could see the bones through his skin. All the bones I—. Mama stopped there.

Papa wouldn't return again after their wedding night, which they spent in the animal shed, on straw trampled during the gathering. The family lore is that then Papa left Spain in '38 and arrived in Moscow. The Party immediately rescued him from the hunger queues. Papa became a sort of small-time provincial commissioner. Fortunately. Four years of silence later, the big war started. There's no place for you here, they told him by letter. Not for you and not for anyone. Here, there is only pain.

When the Nazis left, Papa moved to Dresden. That wasn't until 1946. And only then, when he had a home and a job, did he write to Mama. A letter that was passed hand-to-hand, a letter that traversed the smouldering ruins of Europe. Our future tucked inside that envelope. It was his handwriting, and, to my knowledge, it said: Isabel, come to me. They'll let you know how, don't be afraid, but come. And my mother was afraid, but she went, train by train, until Barcelona. A couple picked her up near Figueres. When they crossed the border, Mama pretended to be sick in the backseat. She kept her eyes closed and heard the couple say something in French. They spent the night on the other side. She didn't sleep. I was awake the whole night, terrified someone was going to break down my door, she said. But nothing happened. A few weeks later, my parents found each other in Dresden, among a small community of Spaniards. It was like a make-believe village: you will be blacksmith; you can be a cook. When they asked me what I knew how to do, I shook my head: I'm a teacher, Mama said. And that was it. The Party helped the families settle into little houses grouped together. There were children of Spanish exiles who didn't speak their parents' language and danced the *Kalinka Maya*. I was born

The Other Side

Fifteen

Black September, White Dress

Backnang, 1972

THEY CALLED ME *THE SPANISH GIRL*. ONLY when there was more time for conversation could I try to explain that I was German, but that my parents—. But I—. But Berlin—. The other side—. Johannes would signal to me with a nod of his head. And I'd stop talking.

That first year, I lived upstairs in Johannes's parents' house in Plattenwald. I had my own entrance. A flower-laden exterior staircase to the lofted second floor. Up there, old timber beams, dark wood strips halfway up the walls, little metal decorations, a big bed, desk, a bathroom. Johannes set up a television right away. From one of the windows, a succession of pitched roofs, the whole town a perfect painting. The other window had a small balcony where I could sit when the weather was nice; its view was of cultivated fields as far as the eye could see. There were horses in one of the meadows. I never saw them gallop. I ate breakfast, lunch and dinner downstairs every day and Johannes would come upstairs and we would talk and drink beer. Some nights, Johannes fell asleep naked on the bed. But at some point before dawn, he would get dressed and go to his own room. I could never fall asleep on my own. The silence of that house was excruciating, when he left me before I was in bed. The dream train on its tracks, rolling by with images of Papa and Mama and my life on the other side of the wall.

A memory: one night that first summer, when I couldn't sleep, I opened the door, went downstairs, and walked out behind the house. I went as far as the river Murr. I crossed the wooden bridge and sat on the other side,

The nights were long. Especially in the winter. At four in the afternoon, dusk fell and people moved indoors. Some evenings we would go for a beer, after Johannes finished work and came home from football practice. In the glow of lamplight, people drank and got drunk in silence. All of the bars were wooden, with carved and lacquered stools, orderly and bright. It didn't look at all like the scene of a good time. One night, I got drunk as well. Johannes also had too much. And we kissed in front of everyone: me, my back against the bar, the wooden edge almost at my shoulder, his hands leaning on it, on either side of my trembling body. He bent over me, I watched as his fringe fell over my eye, and then it was his mouth and all the air and all that was promised, and his body covered mine at last. In that moment, none of it existed: not the wall, the reprisals, the young *Wessis* dancing around us, *Hey babe, take a walk on the wild side*, accusation in their eyes, she's from over there, she's from over there. It didn't exist. Only guilt – a poison administered in short, continuous doses – rendered me motionless and left me quiet, eyes empty. Back in the loft, Johannes wanted to take my clothes off but I couldn't move. I started to cry and my stomach retched everything up.

At four in the morning, his mother prepared a fruit tea in the green kitchen and asked me to sit with her. The house smelled like sweet fruit, but the tea was sour. You'll get used to it, she said. But I stirred in honey. You'll get fat. Katia, you must—, if you—, you'll see—, when you're a mother. She asked about my family, but not really. My studies, but not really. University really is something else over there, don't you think? The people don't work like we do here. I never really managed to get anywhere with her. She brushed away anything upsetting with a wave of her hands. Stop, stop. And so I did. That perfect woman and her upturned blue eyes and hair that fell over her shoulder, ribbons to match her outfit. That woman who picked fruit from her own trees to make her own jam, who planned meals with caloric precision, pulchritude, order, *Kehrwoche*, who had kept all the embroidered clothing from when her children were small, organized in cardboard boxes: Björn: 0–3 months. And the cradle carved from Alpen wood by a great-grandfather, in which three generations had slept. In her kitchen, everything was green: the table-cloth, the cushion covers, the picture frames, the salt shaker, the dishes, even the light, filtering through the trees.

With Johannes's father, I barely managed to speak beyond the first day. He told me I was welcome and looked me over. He was often not at home, and I was long up in my room by the time he arrived back from work. Once, he tossed a few books on politics on to the kitchen table in front of me, it's all in there, I expect your head could use some truths. Like almost all Germans his age, he had been in the second war and everything that came before. It left him with a limp. He was in Russia. And though I asked Johannes many times about that part of his father's life, he always refused to say any more about it. That doesn't matter now, he said, it's in the past.

There were no fences around the houses in the village, they opened to the street and only neatly trimmed hedges marked where one's private property ended and another's began. Nobody put a foot out of place. One evening, I was sitting on the front steps when a young couple with a child stopped in front of me.

They told us you're from over there. So are we. *Ossis*. A big space opened in my heart for Max, Frieda, and little Michael that night. Several years before, they had escaped through Tunnel 29. Back when the Stasi was still ignorant of the tunnel that East Berlin students had dug under the Bernauer Straße. Many were the afternoons that I crossed the street to knock on their door. She was a redhead in those days, her eyes so light she could barely open them in the sunlight. She had a round face, a single open-seamed coat, and a dark green scarf she had knitted herself. She was my second real friend. Sometimes we lost track of time, reminiscing about our Berlin, that little patch of land under siege. She would open a bottle of wine and, since we didn't often drink, the alcohol would loosen our tongues. Once, we even went so far as to sing the *Auferstanden aus Ruinen*, the East German national anthem. When Max got home, he joined in. Crazy women, he said, and brought out another bottle of wine. Max was a literature teacher. I only heard him speak about the East on a few occasions. We came here because I wanted to read, he said. Truly. He was dark-haired, like me, and it seemed every time he opened his mouth it was always to say something pertinent. When we first got here, he spent weeks in the library, Frieda told me. He barely set foot inside the house. He still has *1984* on his nightstand, he bought it in the village bookshop the minute we arrived. He took me straight there with our suitcases, before we even moved in.

There were times when I simply sat at their kitchen table as she fixed dinner and the boy played on the rug. Then she would turn on the twinkling lights that wound around the shelves, and we would sit across the table from one another and drink our coffee in silence. Each shouldering her own burden, until its weight bent our heads so low that one of us would be obliged to end the visit. I should go. Or, I have to give Michael a bath. Those were the worst days, the days I went home with my flesh hot from remembering, from all the unanswerable questions: what was my family doing? What had I done?

Johannes and I got married a year and a half after I arrived. They held the wedding in the village's

Protestant church. When you entered, two pieces of paper indicated in which pews guests should sit. No one had thought it through. On the right, Johannes's family, father, mother, siblings, grandparents, uncles, friends from school and university, neighbours. The perfect family tree. On my side, Max, Frieda, and little Michael. Empty rows behind them. I'm not sure why he parted his hair down the middle and wore that ridiculous bow tie that took up his entire neck. I'm not sure why I could hardly look at him throughout the whole ceremony, why the only thing I could see was that silver bow gleaming under his face. I signed my name to the marriage certificate. And that's when the knot formed in my throat and Johannes tried to loosen it with his words, don't worry, they're here with you, in here, and he took my hand and placed it on his chest in an unsettling paternal gesture. But no one was there inside. And then came the mild hurrahs of the reception to follow.

In one corner of the banquet hall, a muted television transmitted coverage of the Munich Olympics. Germany hadn't hosted the games since Berlin under the Nazis, and they had opened their stadiums to the world in order to erase that image of their country. Those were days of national pride.

We were given many gifts: a camera, a cuckoo clock brought from Freiburg and topped with a pair of enormous squirrels, whose wire I cut to avoid waking at dawn, a set of crystal glassware that would break over time, just as we broke, and a honeymoon in the Black Forest, courtesy of Herr Zeigler. One of my strongest memories from the wedding is a photograph we took with his football team. The two of us in the middle of the big group, him smiling like a maniac and me, overwhelmed by the party and smothered in white satin.

We were too tired to even look at each other on our wedding night. He turned on the TV and we heard the news that Palestinian terrorists had kidnapped and murdered eleven members of the Israeli Olympic delegation and a German police officer.

Germany didn't suspend the games.

In this country, what mattered was to keep going.

Sixteen

Nobody Likes to Dance the Lipsi

Backnang, 1974

MY FATHER NAMED ME KATIA BECAUSE IT WAS a Russian name. It sounds the same in Russian, German, and Spanish, he told my mother. Just in case. And there was nobody else for them to convince.

Johannes said my name often, in the beginning. Katia. Drawing out the *i*. This hair of yours is so dark. The loneliness of the afternoon, the pain, would briefly abandon me then and I'd let him stroke me like a small, orphaned animal. But over time he stopped and simply called me Kat. My hair grew lighter, as well. Over time, and streak by streak.

We moved to a house in a new row of buildings in the town centre. Modern constructions were cropping up among the old houses with their exposed wooden beams, and one knew that the war had destroyed whatever had stood before. On a smaller scale, Johannes reconstructed the home of his childhood. He took charge of liaising with all the labourers. We had a small garden with an old chestnut tree and a white maple. Our first piece of land. When I finally set foot there for the first time, I saw he'd left nothing for me to do. A home is also made up of the view from its windows, and from that house, there wasn't much to see. Windows with café shutters, colourful pinwheels in their flowerpots. None of it looked alive.

In the spring of 1974, we were invited to a barbeque at the home of one of our old neighbours. They invited the whole street. We went with Johannes's parents. He had been in the city that morning and brought clothes back for me. Wear this. A bias-cut shirtdress: a full-skirt and colourful checked fabric, cinched at the waist with a red leather belt.

We ate and drank while the children played in the sandpit and meat cooked slowly on the grill. There were bratwurst and two racks of pork ribs, *Kartoffelsalat, Fleischkäse, Kässpätzle*, giant *Knödel* and an innumerable variety of rolls and breads. I took a pretzel and spread it with butter. Thick flakes of salt dissolved on my tongue. No one tried my goulash.

After the meal, the hosts set up chairs in a circle and offered everyone Schnapps. Would you be so kind? Trudi the hostess said to Björn, handing him a guitar. Johannes's brother shook his head with false modesty but finally conceded and struck up a Bavarian tune. When he finished, everyone clapped. But Björn just smiled and strummed the first chords of '*Kein schöner Land*.' Everyone sang along. I had never heard it sung before. *No country more beautiful in this time, as ours here, both far and near, where we can find one another, under the lime trees at eventide.* I looked at Max and then at Frieda and both raised their little glass of Schnapps. Frieda winked. When they finished the song, all the guests toasted each other effusively. Johannes looked at me and looked at my hands and made a gesture with his head. I raised them up to my face and clapped weakly.

The afternoon light was growing weak. Trudi thanked Björn and took back the guitar, the noise might bother the neighbours. Freidrich was fined last week, she explained, just because his dog barked for five minutes at sunrise. There was silence, then. Johannes stood, the sound of ice cubes tinkling at the bottom of his glass.

That was when one of the neighbourhood women turned to me:

Do you like our Germany, then?

Yes, I said. I've been here a while now.

But there must be things you miss, she said.

Yes, there are, I answered.

Oh, yes? Johannes's father intervened. And what do you miss? Do tell, Katia.

I don't know, things.

But you must know what, my father-in-law insisted. We'd love to hear.

This isn't necessary, Papa, Johannes said.

In a moment of courage, I stood my ground with Johannes's father.

My friends, I said. Friendships are different over there, stronger. I'm not saying that they aren't strong here, as well.

Frieda was taking a sip of Schnapps and I watched as she tried to conceal her whole face behind the tall, skinny glass; I couldn't tell whether she was dying of embarrassment or stifling laughter. It was 1974 and the GDR had finally been recognized as a nation. The two Germanies had signed an agreement permitting travel – in exceptional family situations – between the two countries. But not in my case. I had fled. The door was barred.

My father-in-law leaned on his cane and got to his feet. He approached me, close enough that I sensed the menace, but not so close that the others couldn't hear what he said.

Well, go back, then, if you miss them so much. You'll see how happily they receive you. You'd be doing your family a favour. Or hadn't you thought of that, dear Katia?

No one spoke.

But suddenly, there was an abrupt movement: Max, normally so circumspect, got up and walked across the ring of chairs to where I sat. He performed an exaggerated bow and held out his hand. I took it. And maybe it was the effects of the alcohol, or the impending dusk, but Max launched into an off-key Lipsi. I didn't try to stop him. We danced, two steps to the left, turn, two to the right, turn, before the incredulity of the other guests. The dress from Johannes twirled, lifted to mid-thigh, and even though I refused to look at him, I could feel his words inside my head, every single sentence. Ultimately, he was the one who put a stop to it. The one who dropped his glass on the wooden table and said don't be ridiculous. Who put me in the car and didn't say another word until later that night. Who shouted about just how many marks he had negotiated to get me out of my country and how many calls his own father had made to get false papers and to pay that man who hardly spoke the entire journey as he drove me across the whole of Czechoslovakia in the old Trabant.

When they named our first daughter Theresa, I said nothing.

It's tradition to name her after her paternal grand-mother, Johannes said.

Fine. I had no argument to make.

But then I thought about how Theresa was a Spanish name too. And I smiled at the baby beside our bed, fast asleep in the old wooden cradle.

Seventeen

Brézhnev's Kiss

Backnang, 1979

THAT RIVER, THE MORAVA, CUT MY LIFE IN two. I knew it before I reached the other side, before I ever set foot in the West. Everything I knew was abandoned over the black water, where my mother's Russian hat would for ever lie, devoured by moss and mud. The rest, soaked. I didn't allow myself to think too much about all that, and much less about the consequences my decision might have had. When a memory snuck through the blur of the routine, the baby, the flowers in the windows, the house, I pushed it away, I turned on the television or went to do the shopping. It was as if I had no family at all, once inside these borders. I was country-less, and orphaned too. As if I hadn't walked every single one of East Berlin's streets, and all that remained of the young woman reared on Socialism was a housewife with little or no interest in proving anything to anybody. But above all, I needed to not provoke more truth-telling by Johannes or his father, no more shouting to remind me where my people could still be found, making me wonder if they had suffered, or think who else might have noticed my absence. Because, if that were the case . . . Katia had disappeared. Those were chilling thoughts, and like someone pushing their glass away when they'd had enough, I shoved them aside. To the edge of the table. The edge of my life. Stop there. Over time, I yanked my attachments out at the root.

Sometimes, I read articles in the newspaper and tried to convince myself that none of it mattered to me. I followed the news, but only like an armchair historian with an amateur's interest in whether or not that place, the East, was headed for collapse. Never on tenterhooks, never in suspense.

And so it fell further and further into the past, watery and submerged.

Those were the days of détente. People stopped asking themselves what was going to happen. There were no answers. No debate. Europe's history like a deflated worm, the air gone out of it. No one seemed to care now that the country was divided, that thousands of families still had one half on either side. That my city was still surrounded by a cement wall, armed soldiers dressed in green and posted in towers. People had stopped making fun of the East. The people who had been disappeared weighed heavily on no one. It was the post-post-war and the West was living the German dream, holding its head high, while the East was crumbling before the eyes of the world.

Throughout the whole Soviet Bloc, uprisings broke out. The Prague Spring was just the first to say *Enough*. The Politburo sent its red army to the satellite states. And the president of the GDR's Central Committee, Erich Honecker, fearing for his besieged State, welcomed the USSR. The manoeuvres were clumsy. The balance, destabilized. The new world witnessed Brézhnev and Honecker's unexpected kiss on the lips. And so the Socialist leaders shored up the country's division, affirming on television for all to see that nothing was over, nothing had ended. Lifting the spirits of our pitiable bureaucrats and delivering a new and unexpected source of comedy to the West.

But it was, after all, the age of consumerism and the *desire* to consume, on both sides of the Iron Curtain. The 1970s were coming to an end, and we had bought our second car, traded our wooden furniture for glass pieces with clean lines and mirrored doors, rugs and long velvet couches, and when my little country celebrated its thirtieth birthday, I had been in the Federal Republic of Germany for eight years.

If the war was cold, I was frozen stiff.

Theresa turned three that year. We celebrated her birthday at her grandparents' house. I don't know why, it wasn't as if we didn't have a home of our own. They have a bigger garden, Johannes said. So what? Well, yeah, so what? When we arrived, her grandmother still had the *Strudel* in the oven and the whole house was filled with the sweet smell of golden apples softening on their bed of cinnamon and raisins. They'd hung streamers and balloons up in the yard. A table in the corner for the pile of presents. Once she had blown out her three candles, the applause still crackling with happy wishes, Theresa started on the gifts, her little hands shredding the paper. She grabbed a box with a toy inside, shook it without opening it, left it on the ground seconds later. It took her five minutes to tear through all of them. Then she stood up, glanced at me, and ran off after one of her little friends.

The evening came to a close and the guests began to leave. On the porch, Theresa dozed on her father's chest. Her blonde hair fell over his shoulder. He was talking football with his brother, legs planted wide, a glass of beer balanced in his hand. My mother-in-law was folding bits of wrapping paper she had salvaged, smoothing it against her chest. She didn't look up. And I was still clutching my soft drink, walking along the hedge that bordered the back of the garden. The wall of cypress rose toward the sky, towering over me. I pressed my hand against the dense darkness.

The phone was ringing inside. Johannes's father went to answer. I started collecting plates and bringing leftovers to the kitchen. I paused on the porch and turned to look back at the garden. Always something so melancholy about a house after a party, I thought. I stepped through the door and saw my father-in-law inside his office. He gestured to me, come in, come here. He was standing next to his desk. I had only been in there once, chasing after Theresa. The lamplight shone from behind him, casting his shadow towards me. He held the phone as if it burned his hand, as if he wanted nothing to do with any information that device could possibly transmit. His other hand gripped his cane, supporting all his weight. I went to him slowly. I put down the plates and reached out my hand. He stepped forward and brought his face very close to mine. I stood motionless as Herr Ziegler kissed my forehead. He laid the phone in my hands like it was a wounded bird. I felt the cold of the Bakelite against my cheek. My father-in-law didn't leave the room. He put both hands on the knob of his cane and lowered his head. On the other end of the line, the same sound of the breath I'd slept next to for the first twenty years of my life.

Katia. Papa is dead.

My sister's words.

That's all she said.

The line went dead.

The tower of dirty plates on the desk toppled to the floor. The three little candles on the rug, globs of cake that left a stain.

my waist. I washed Theresa's little face, leaning her over the sink. I wet the comb and traced a straight line, dividing her scalp in two. Then I leaned on the counter top with crossed arms and watched her drink from her mug by herself. Her head just barely peeking out above the tablecloth. Before she left each day, I straightened the square satchel on her back and gave her a kiss. By that time, Johannes had already backed the car out of the garage. The girl climbed in – always in the back seat, right behind her father, the duplicate sets of blue eyes, the grown man, the little girl – and she waved to me with her small hand. He fiddled with the rear-view mirror. Then I shut the door and smelled the soap and cologne and chill air of the early morning inside the house. I switched on the dim light over the kitchen table and some-times tried to read. I almost always closed the book, distracted, and flipped through circulars of advertise-ments and discounts. Once the sun rose high enough to reach our windows, I switched off the lamp and everything from earlier – the bustle, the girl, the jar of shoe polish left on the table, the crumbs of dark bread – seemed to belong to a different life.

The town was different too, at that time of day. Other people went off to their jobs or their schools and the streets were just skeletons, bare bones, and those of us walking them in that half-light were like stagehands, setting the scene for the moment the curtain would rise and the real actors would appear. There was a certain complicity among us, citizens of those mornings. The strange camaraderie of the excluded, those of us who would not get on the train but remain behind on the platform, a sorry gathering that didn't actually strike anybody as particularly good or bad.

For years, I mourned my father's death from the other side of the wall, in absolute solitude. When someone dies and there's no burial, no funeral, the condolences peter out more quickly than usual. The people who don't have memories of that person, who haven't seen the expressionless body, swiftly forget that you were someone who once had a father, and that father was a man with a dream, with dreams, with furies and desires, a man eternally pierced by an absurd nostalgia for a place that had never really been. And so people come and go from your house like nothing has happened. And you pretend it doesn't matter now. Because your decision was ill-conceived. Hasty, premature. Impulsive. And you don't know whether he had cried at night, for his daughter, for his family, for socialism. For himself. Papa. Papa, I said when I was alone. For all the times I would never call him that again.

It was after that, after Martina's call, that I stopped answering the phone with our last name, Ziegler, and simply said Katia instead. I waited for her. But Martina never called again. And I began to wonder how the call that afternoon had even been possible. Katia, Papa is dead, my name at the start of that sentence, Katia, Katia, Papa is dead, my sister's words, Papa is dead. Four words. How did she have our number, my in-laws' phone number, what terror had she confronted in order to tell me, and why did she do it? Because she hung up. She hadn't waited, hadn't waited to know more. Katia. How much did she know about me? Papa is dead. She gave me nothing but that piece of information, information that dragged me down like a stone, into a mire of disordered thoughts, black and dark.

I would no longer be a father's daughter.

His daughter.

I stopped joining the other mothers after picking up Theresa from the *kinder*. I couldn't stand their conversations. On sale, two for one, sinus infection, the novel by, a pinch of salt. On rare occasions I would pick up Theresa and, to kill some time in the afternoon, take her to visit Max and Frieda. I wanted her to know where we came from, the both of us. The journeys her family had had to undertake, batted about by the decisions of others, so that they could sit there at a table, spreading jam on bread. And Frieda would look at me with worry, Katia, are you all right? I always said yes. My depression had its own routines. I wrote letters, interminable letters that I would never send: to Julia, my mother, Martina. I stopped going out in the mornings and got back into bed. I didn't spend time in the sun, and the roots of my hair grew dark again. I stopped doing the shopping, stopped watering our flowers, stopped organizing the closets and photographs.

One evening, Johannes left work late and when he got home our daughter was still sitting in front of the TV. Dinner wasn't ready. There was nothing to eat in the house. And that man – with whom I'd lived for a third of my life by that point – stood stock still and stared at me. Cold blue eyes, black suit on his body. Both of us ridiculous in our costumes. He started yelling. Where are you, Kat. Where are you, Katia. Katia. He switched off the TV and took the girl and left the house. When they returned, I was sitting on the edge of the bed. I heard them come in, the light in Theresa's room switch on, the toothbrush, the faucet, and the light switching off again. The man who had shouted at me came into our room. He didn't look at me. He opened the door to the bathroom and disappeared. I heard the water falling on his body.

Johannes left the bathroom and stopped in the middle of the room. Naked. He didn't look at me. He was simply there, all his weight motionless on the blue rug. Two legs holding up a body. A kind of challenge, an invitation. I was made to understand that I was the one who would have to change the night's trajectory. I looked at his hips, at the space his arms left along his torso. I got off the bed and went to him. I knew I should undress. And I did, very slowly. My clothes fell at our feet. He lifted his eyes from the floor but didn't make a single move. I was still too. His eyes opened unusually wide. I moved closer. I could brush my breasts against his chest. We took each other's measure. My hair touched his chin. That was who we were. This is where I end and you begin, here. Two bodies in contradiction. Johannes grabbed me hard. We held each other for several minutes. And then everything unfolded slowly. Too slowly.

Eight months later, our second daughter was born early. When they laid her on my chest, she was a small, dark animal covered in grease and blood. She wiped at her own face with little swats of her hand. She opened her eyes right away and I saw they were like mine. They're black, I said to Johannes.

Nineteen

Countries That No Longer Exist

1989

HE HADN'T SAID A WORD. IT WAS THE MIDDLE
of July before Johannes mentioned taking a trip. We
hadn't discussed it. Too much effort. We'll stay here.
We'll take walks in the woods and grill on the lake-
shore of the Diebachstausee at the weekend. Summer
plans, done and done.

But one July afternoon, Johannes opened the front
door at midday, much earlier than usual.

Why are you home so early?

We're going somewhere.

Where?

South, he said. I'm not going to tell you anything else.

Are we going in the car? Is it far? Theresa asked.

Yes. And we'll leave just as soon as you're all ready. From the doorway, he looked at me and smiled, inhaled. It looked as if he was balancing on his tiptoes. I'll check the tyres.

How, I wondered, how had this man been capable of something improvised like this? But I realized that no, this wasn't a spontaneous trip, it had all been planned carefully. Kilometre by kilometre, more than likely. I summoned my will and put on shoes, packed clothes in a sports bag, took a suitcase for the girls down from the top shelf in the closet.

We set out around three o'clock in the afternoon. Johannes was in the car with a map open on the dashboard, drawing straight lines in pencil. He started when he saw us on the front steps – as if he'd seen three ghosts – and quickly tucked the map away in the glove box.

Theresa and Isabel were restless, bickering over small bits of territory on the backseat. When I turned to look at them, surprised by their silence an hour and a half later, they were fast asleep, curled against the car doors. I studied Johannes's profile – the blue eyes behind his sunglasses, liquid orbs, water. Fine lines branching from the corners of his eyes toward his temples, a show of his satisfaction.

Where are we going? Tell me.

No, he said, simply. He didn't take his eyes off the road.

I leaned against the window and slept too. I didn't wake until we were at the border. I sat up and smoothed my hands over my hair and skirt. An officer approached the window. Johannes handed him four passports. The man asked us to open the trunk. We watched as he briefly looked in, then closed it and motioned us on. We had crossed the border only twice since 1971. The first time, when we were traveling from Munich to the south one Christmas, Johannes had insisted on showing me the castle at Neuschwanstein. You'll love it, you've never seen anything like it, he said. But he took a wrong turn and, suddenly, at the end of the road and flanked by five feet of snow on either side, we saw the sign: Austria. It was the first time I'd left the Federal Republic of

Germany since arriving, but my second time in Austria. We crossed the border without any trouble. We drank hot chocolate in a small town, pressing our frozen bodies together and touching under the table until we earned looks of disapproval. We left before nightfall. The error had been so unexpected, so sudden, that I hadn't had time to be afraid. On the second occasion, we went to Switzerland with Johannes's family. We had taken the same road we were driving on now, but had got off at the exit toward Basel. We passed the turn for the Swiss town and I ruled it out as Johannes's destination.

It was close to six in the evening when we crossed into France. The sun was low. It shone in our eyes and the glare made driving almost impossible. The landscape was distorted, like a blurry photograph. Johannes left the highway and we stopped in Mulhouse. We're just spending the night, he said. A stopover. My eyes widened. France. When Theresa and Isabel woke up, they were thrilled to be in a different country.

The whole time in Mulhouse, Johannes went on about the Dreyfus *affaire*, dear Captain Alfred, an early-century European legend born in Mulhouse. I couldn't manage to pay attention for more than a minute. I had no idea Johannes knew anything about history. It was the first time I'd heard him talk about it and I barely listened. I concentrated on taking care of the girls: pulling their hair back from their faces, helping them with dinner, lying between them as they fell asleep. What Johannes didn't tell the girls, or me, and which I only realized once we were sitting at a bar in the square, under the painted porticos of houses that had been perfectly restored after years of wars and annexations and surrender, *Sachsenhausen, Buchenwald, Dachau*, drinking Alsatian wine and eating cheese, what Johannes left out of his story and what ripped my night in two, *Chelmno, Treblinka, Auschwitz*, is that next to those mountains, wild, high, *Nacht und Nebel*: a concentration camp and the deaths of thousands of members of the French Resistance.

The next morning we set off with full stomachs. Johannes was in good spirits but I was tense. I stopped following his conversation, the banter to help the kilometres pass more quickly. I was quiet, and I sought something in the landscape, my thoughts directed outside the car as we drove deeper and deeper into France.

I barely spoke at lunch. But then, near Le Boulou –
the south unfolding before us, ever-warmer air, the
deepening darkness to our left and the Mediterranean
wind that struck the coast – I saw a sign on the road.
Had it said Portbou?

Johannes, did that say Portbou?

I don't know, he said. I didn't see. Do you want
me to turn around?

No.

But my father filled my mind, my nerves, my whole
body: listen, Katia, our war didn't end in '39, as some
say, there was still Portbou, a little town at the edge of
the sea, practically on the French border. Thousands
of Spaniards fled to exile through there. Thousands,
Katia, all through the mountains, along the beach,
with just the clothes on their backs. That was the
longest war. That war is not over.

Are we going to cross the border? I asked Johannes.

Yes.

Which border, Mama? Theresa shouted, excited.
No one answered her.

Did you girls know that there's a king where we're
going? Johannes said.

What do you mean, a king?

A king, with a queen. And princesses.

Theresa, interest piqued, stuck her head between the front seats, and I really regretted that I hadn't explained anti-Semitism and the second war to her back in Mulhouse. In truth, I knew that was as irrational as demanding that Johannes have the decency not to discuss my parents' country: he was talking just to talk, entertaining us with his four misremembered facts, and besides, to whom should he show his respect? To me, as German as he was, to my family, to the Spanish Republic, to the thousands of exiles in Portbou? What did he know about any of that? When had he ever even asked? The knot of places I was made of, the confusion he felt toward me. Johannes, rooted so deeply in the green meadows of Backnang, so fair, clear, the very image of Germany, and I, the daughter of this place, born in that one, dark, fugitive, a lie. But he could at least start explaining to our daughters why we had come, why he had decided to make this journey south, crossing the whole of France, reciting thousands of anecdotes about each town we passed. All to bring me face to face with a country I didn't know except through my parents and a handful of photographs. *La República*, Katia, *el fascismo*, Katia. Because if my parents' Spain no longer existed, then the country they taught me to hate with virulence, the country that allowed its dictator to die in a warm bed, to draw his last breath snug under the covers, that country was gone now too.

I crossed into Spain for the first time. Something had hold of my lungs, I could barely breathe. Twenty minutes later, Johannes stopped beside a big old stone house. We'll sleep here tonight. A girl looked out from the upstairs window and waved to us. We waved back. Then he put his arm around my waist and pulled me to him. Are you happy? I looked at him and smiled, tugging on the sleeping Isabel's limp arm in the backseat. We had dinner with the owners. They spoke Spanish with some difficulty, to my surprise, but we managed to understand each other. They grated tomatoes over enormous slices of bread splattered with olive oil and cut wedges of watermelon. The table was long and the whole family seemed happy to have us there. Johannes spent the meal asking me to translate every single word. I was

ground was wet and streams ran in ditches alongside the road. We passed an abandoned house clinging to its foundation. I told Johannes to stop and he pulled over and parked on the shoulder. We had yet to drive down into the village. The girls stayed in the car but Johannes got out and hugged me from behind. He wasn't the person I should have been with, the first time I saw that place. He left me and started down the road. He crossed to the other side and called to me, Katia, look. An old village washhouse. A small plaque: 1915, in red brushstrokes. My mother had almost certainly been here, I thought. I walked over to Johannes, running my hand along the stone banister. In the troughs, old rust and new filth. Johannes took me by the shoulders and spun me to face him. He stepped back and snapped a picture. There, I thought. Katia at her most forlorn, entering her parents' village.

At the bottom of a small winding road, we passed a sign marking the entrance to Dos Aguas. All the streets ran either uphill or down. They were so narrow that even the lowest houses loomed imposing and white. The July midday sun battered the faces of the buildings. Johannes parked in the plaza. We explored every hidden corner in that village. I watched, annoyed, as Johannes and the girls ran about, played hide-and-seek in the doorways, made a scene. Isabel fell. She came to me, crying, palms face up. A woman watched us out her window. Johannes assured her everything was fine, waving his arm to downplay the commotion.

This is your fault, I said to him, as I poured water on a tissue and wiped away the dirt and blood.

We sat outside on a terrace and drank beer and ordered roasted vegetables and fish. The girls wouldn't try a bite. A puddle of yellow oil stained the plate. Everything was dirty.

You should ask someone.

Ask them what?

About your family. Maybe somebody around here is related to you.

Right.

Come on, ask.

Just stop, Johannes. What do you want me to say? *Hola*, I'm Katia, you've never seen me before in your life, but I'm sure my father's story will sound familiar. He escaped to Germany and I decided to abandon him, just like that. One day, I just left.

Johannes motioned for me to quieten down. The girls were watching me with wide eyes, pieces of bread in their little hands. A young couple looked over from the table next to us. We were just four Germans, arguing about something more important than dessert under the Dos Aguas sun.

It's fine, I told them. It's fine.

By the time they all woke, I had already picked up our clothes and packed the suitcases.

I don't want to be here any more.

We left early, heading to the coast for a few days by the sea. No one had asked who we were or what we were doing in Dos Aguas, my mother's village, my father's village. No one had answered: that's the communist's daughter.

That autumn, under the blows of pickaxes and hammers wielded by thousands of Berliners, the wall came down.

Twenty

Atomic Number 28

Backnang, 1990

THE WORST OF IT WASN'T THE ROUTINE. IT wasn't the falling out of love. The worst of it all wasn't that I, in the deepest part of myself, resented Johannes for removing me from what had been my life. The worst weren't his attempts, his efforts. It wasn't Capitalism, that system of selling your time. Nor was it the education my daughters were getting and the distance I felt from them. The songs, the *Schültute*, all the children's birthdays I had to attend, the same questions, the promising future. For me, the truly terrible thing was the calm that followed every argument, that emptiness on the days when, in the end, Johannes went off to work and I spent hours in absolute solitude, until the night. The days I hoped he wouldn't come home early and fantasized about the demise of everything I had. When, after each new wound, there was nothing that could heal me entirely and a tepid tedium settled between us: me, hanging off the edge, and him with less and less time to give us. And neither one had the strength to talk. We were worn out, him on the outside and me all over. How many times can two trains crash head-on? How long until one engine says I can't, not again, because, if we do, there won't be a next time, there will be nothing left for you to hit. There had always been something inside, in my gut, in my heart, a whisper that I had made my choice, it had been my gamble to upend my whole life and the lives of those that loved me. And this was my punishment. To live without my home-land. Like my mother had.

It rained that morning. After dropping the girls at school, both oblivious to the collapse around them, I turned on the radio in the bedroom and got into the shower. It was the 4 October, 1990.

> 'After precisely forty-one years, 14,971 days, the Democratic Republic of Germany is history. Its 16 million inhabitants now form part of the German Federated Republic: a new country has been born. 79 million people can now say that they are Germans, and nothing else.'

Who would write our country's history? Germans from this side? Johannes hadn't slept at home that night. It had been a long time since we had slept in the same bed. I prefer you not to be home tomorrow morning, I told him. We should leave from different places to do what we're going to do. I wore dark colours; I felt I had to dress the part. I slipped several documents into a folder. In the bathroom mirror, I tried to erase traces of the night: few hours of sleep and a feeling of dread. I studied my face: the same long fringe as always, the same sharp nose, the small chin. I thought things like, now you have to find a job, how lonely the night is, once the girls are in bed.

I thought about my parents, about them both, their names and surnames, about whether they had ever wanted to leave, both of them, whether they had ever lived at odds. Whether they had wanted to sleep in separate beds but got into the same one at the end of each day nonetheless and turned away or made love face-to-face. They too had lived outside their country. Then I thought about all the things we hadn't had. And all that we did. And about all the women I'd met over the years living in Backnang and the years I'd lived on the other side. *Gleiche Rechte.* Equal rights.

'The Brandenburg Gate was witness to the celebration. Before this monument, once a symbol of division, more than a million Germans rejoiced that we are now a larger, more populous country, unified at long last. Yesterday will be a pivotal date for our nation. Germany has taken its sovereignty back from the victors of the Second World War. The painful division is behind us.'

It was still too early to go into the city when I left the house. I went for a coffee next to the S-Bahn station. Takeaway, I said. I walked carefully, the hot liquid between my hands. The cold weather hadn't yet arrived, but after just a few minutes the coffee had cooled enough to sip. I felt it slide down my throat. I had barely eaten in days. The train pulled in, its windows reflecting my image back to me. Blurry. Clutching a paper cup. I couldn't move. For the first time, my impulse was to stay where I was, not move ahead. I couldn't board the train. I let it pass: my reflection sliced horizontally as window after window sped by. The next train arrived ten minutes later. I sat across from a young woman. She was probably on her way to the university. I looked at my feet. I thought about the university in Berlin. My studies, half-finished then abandoned. Maybe I could start up again. Would those years of schooling count for something, now that this was one country? I supposed that they would. Now I was living on a narrow peak, which I walked with the care of a tightrope walker, terrified of falling on either side. But it was too late: the place I'd once had to return to no longer existed. Our country had underestimated the power that rules everything, and battled the most ferocious laws of Capitalism with intolerance as its shrewdest strategy. And everything we had been taught, absolutely everything, was worthless. I was an orphaned girl whose father had died. And nobody was coming to protect me. And I had doubts, then. I doubted whether or not I should get off at the next station, turn back, tell Johannes, I'll stay. Together. Reunified. But by then I could already see the Neckar River flowing under the train tracks. I was entering the city.

'It will be complicated, but we will all work so that our country becomes the great power it is. When the celebratory candles go out, I'm sure there will be new differences, not for nothing, millions of Germans have been educated for decades under a totalitarian regime; one can't learn from one day to the next how to live together in a democratic system.'

I signed the divorce papers. As we were being read the agreements, the girls would live with me, in the family home, I would receive a monthly payment of—, the father has the right to—, I rolled the old fountain pen between my fingers. I ran my finger over my name. The pen had survived everything with me. I remembered something from Chemistry class in secondary school: nickel's location on the periodic table. Ni. Atomic number 28. Highly durable, high boiling and fusion points, good conductor of heat. A different society for a different education. A different education for a different society. Karl Marx. I closed my eyes.

Everything solid had crumbled: the young man who had waited for me, who had pushed back against rules and crossed his country and mine, young Johannes, young Katia. Gone: transformed into the man who left for work and came home and undid his tie so he could breathe more easily, who watched TV and drank a glass of water, lifting his arm high. Johannes I-leave-it-all-for-you, Johannes you-took-everything-from-me. Johannes there-are-no-borders, Johannes the-wall.

'The bars of "The International", played by a few musicians from the East at the base of the Reichstag, sound pathetic now in the midst of such joy, a requiem for a State that has been liquidated.

As our Chancellor stated: dictatorship and denial of freedom have been overcome at last. Today the sun shines on Germany. On both sides. Our country is one in this new autumn. We are part of a united Europe. And Berlin is Berlin again.'

With that signature, I felt I was turning to face in the right direction, that it was what I had to do and the new challenges I would have to confront didn't matter. I was the daughter of an anti-Fascist country, a country that believed in freedom, a strained and impoverished country, rural and safe, and I needed to rebel and get out of this other place somehow and that meant leaving Johannes, our house, our city. I considered that chain of muddled thoughts and looked at him one last time before I did it. I spoke. Johannes. How did we come to this. He signed after me, his head bent low. And I would never be able to remember any other preceding image.

I left the lawyer without really knowing where to go. The streets were filled with remnants from the revelry. Germany was one again. But our flag had not been part of the celebration. I sat on a bench and looked at the papers I'd just been handed. At my name, Katia, at the signature that time and habit had moulded into another woman, what surname would follow that Katia now?

Do you ever think about what it means to be here for ever?

Vaterland

Berlin, summer of 1992

THEY'VE BEEN QUICK. IT'S LIKE EVERYONE
who lived in the city has died and their distant relatives have gone into their homes and dismantled
what there had been of their lives. All they had
saved, treasured for decades, tossed into the streets,
in pieces. How long does it take? How long does it
take to enter a home and swipe anything you could
put a price on. Anything somebody might buy. All
those objects. All those letters. *Lieber Jens, Leiber
Guerlinde.* Purposeless, now. *Grüße aus Leipzig.* All
the names. All the lives. Not the clothes, the armchairs,
the pots that had boiled water, the lamps that had lit
the darkness. That's all they were. Skeletons devoid of

life, a museum in the street in a defunct country: gas masks, medals, toy handcuffs, old wooden boomerangs, uniforms, soldiers' caps the likes of which she's never seen before. Pieces of the wall wrapped in cellophane with certificates of authenticity. The more graffiti, the higher the price. And although Katia's wall had been concrete and grey and only grey, now it was the wall's other side that held real value. And she doesn't recognize the people in the city either. They all look younger than she is, more modern. At any rate, she comes from a town in the south now, too. She stops in front of the stalls set up at the entrance to the train station. Was something of hers among all that stuff? A university ID card, the blue beret. What was left? She approaches one of the stalls. It's different from the others. The goods look Russian: *matryoshka* nesting dolls, arranged large to small, amber stones, Bohemian crystal. She thinks about buying something for the girls. But she closes her eyes and, for a moment, she only wants to stay there in Berlin, behind the wall, sitting in its shadow.

One day and night. That's how long Katia has been in the city. But she feels as if it has been much longer. When she got off the train and took a breath, it was the same city smell as on the other side. When she set off walking, and didn't take a single tram. Because the important places, her father used to say, must be reached on foot, so one is conscious of the journey. She smiles for a moment. Her father. A father.

The whole city looks under construction. Many of the windows have been boarded up or covered with sheets of plastic that swell and deflate like sails in a summer breeze and the buildings in the Mitte have been subjected to modern renovations, ready to be sold as small completely equipped apartments at exorbitant prices for Eastern budgets. On the pavements there are tables and chairs where groups of young people drink beer and chat happily. A small band sings in English, distorting their guitars to a rhythm Katia can't follow. She pauses next to them.

Fresh hired hands drag wheelbarrows over the raised streets. Wooden ladders scale the buildings. Everything else looks off-kilter, as if a hurricane has levelled the city she had known and now they were struggling to rebuild. Streetlights, lamp posts, huge chunks of buildings in the middle of the street. She looks up and a girl is leaning out of the window, half her body outside. She paints the windowsill yellow as her neighbour watches from across the way, leaning on his elbows and smoking with indifference.

It's then Katia realizes she's reached the wall. It's still standing, but fragmented, not continuous. Hunks of bulldozed anti-tank barriers and pieces from dilapidated lorries lie at her feet, and where the brightly lit border crossing had been – the dog and the woman and so many others – a group sits around a table, roasting meat on a BBQ, as if they were camping.

Like a ghost, she wanders through neighbourhoods that have all been occupied: now, the buildings are open laboratories for artists and punks. A new symbol appears on their façades, an *A* inside a circle: the city rebelling against any kind of rule, an adolescent running away from home. Katia, just a shadow moving through the noise. On his statue, they've painted a sign between Lenin's hands: *Keine Gewalt*, no violence.

She turns on to what had been her street and stops at what was once the door that led into their courtyard. Her breath quickens. No door remains, no courtyard. Half of the buildings that made up her neighbourhood have been knocked down. But there, on the corner, a miracle: her building and the one adjacent rise from the middle of the lot, beams exposed, guts of hollow bricks and stone and the layout of the rooms perfectly visible, like a macabre dollhouse. Many of the windows are boarded over. There, their living room. Papa's window, she thinks. It's smaller now, several rows of bricks have reduced it by half. At ground level, piles of rubble, mountains of sand, submerged iron rods, a half-buried Trabi right where the trees had stood, a metal pail with trash heaped high in a balancing act. Katia bends down and touches the dirt. She runs her hand over it, it must be the same dirt, even if it looks darker now. And then she turns and looks up. She thinks about her sister and her mother and whether they are inside, whether they saw the buildings come down, the dust, the ruin, the trees. And she looks at the building's entrance, which appears to be open, and the stairwell with the windows that give on to each landing. *Herr Schmidt, Ekaterina, Alexandra*, and she turns away as she says the names she hasn't uttered in twenty years, because there's a void where their homes had been and it's deeply disturbing, deeply disturbing that they didn't even leave the foundation, not even the roots of the trees, the stone bench, one couldn't fathom that people had lived, loved, died there. She's not sure if she's angry at history, herself, or the new residents of Berlin arriving *en masse* from the West, from the very place she now calls home.

A young couple is leaving the vestibule. The man wears a black V-neck T-shirt and tight pants. The woman has a blunt haircut and a fringe that grazes her lashes. Her hair is dyed coal-black, faded blonde at the roots. A little boy follows them, eating an ice cream cone, distracted. For a moment, it's as if she knows them, or wants to know them, but no. The parents wait in the empty lot for the boy to catch up. Thomas, *komm*. Katia smiles.

She decides not to linger any longer, and enters their building. The stairwell appears to have been painted years ago; no longer grey but pastel blue, though water stains have bloomed again, exactly where they always were. On a first-floor wall, someone has spray-painted *Was den Krieg verschonte, überlebt im*

Sozialismus nicht* in cursive. She stops and considers what those words could mean, but can't quite grasp their significance. She can't, at the moment. Still, she takes out her camera and snaps a picture. The stairwell absorbs the burst of flash. Where the wooden handrail had been, only the hooks are left. A chill creeps from the palm of her hand to her arm, to her neck, and for the first time she wonders if she should go back the way she came, if she shouldn't knock on that door, but what agony, if her mother or sister were to recognize her figure crossing the courtyard that no longer exists, if they were to come downstairs, follow her, a mirage swallowed by the commotion in the street. Not again. And so she continues upwards, step by step, eyes on her feet, one after the other, her sandals – so Western – and she remembers all the times her feet climbed those stairs, her father's feet, the three females behind. And then she is standing before the door. Maybe they moved years ago, maybe no one is left and a stranger has already come and destroyed everything that might have held a memory.

---

* What the war spared, Socialism did not.

Suddenly, Katia is hit with all the times she wondered whether something had happened to them, something from which there would be no return, and why her sister had only been able to call that one time. Never before, and not after. She decides not to dwell, not to rehearse her words. She presses the bell, which doesn't ring. She knocks three times, her fist on the ancient wood. She hears noises coming from the other side.

You took a long time, her sister says, and she says it without taking her eyes off the ground, her feet on the other side of the threshold in a pair of worn shoes, and it seems like the very same wall is rising again right there between them. But Martina moves aside and Katia takes this as an invitation. Martina. She says her name. They stare. They look each other up and down and Katia thinks that her sister, as thin as ever but sturdier, more curves than before, must also notice that Katia's hips have spread as well, and that she has nieces or nephews and that now they're all on the same side. And so Katia succumbs to the impulse to step forward and starts to reach out to pull her sister towards her, but Martina recoils and looks at the floor. She takes a few steps inside the apartment and turns to Katia and tells her to wait before disappearing through the door to their parents' bedroom. Katia drags over one of the chairs, the same chairs, and sits. She looks all around her and closes her eyes and wishes the walls would reveal to her the pain caused by her flight, but there's no response and she senses that not a single one of the times she has imagined the day her parents returned to find her gone, never to return, could come close to the desolation they must have lived through, sitting around the family table. The floor is different, as is the kitchen, it's been updated, they stripped the wallpaper. A radiator is mounted on the wall. But the light is the same. The living room is smaller, they've closed part of it off, put up a door. Katia looks up and sees the same window that caught her eye from down below.

The floor creaks and it's her sister in the doorway, pushing a wheelchair. I was getting her ready, she says. Katia gets to her feet and looks at her mother, hunched, her hair is short and white now but she has the same sunken dark eyes, her two hands, bones and veins and the hollow wedding band on her finger. She goes to her, her mother still hasn't looked at her, and her sister says do you know who this is and her mother says no, and looks to Martina and says no again. She asks if it's her sister, Carola. No, Martina says, look carefully, Mama, you know who it is. No. Katia is crying but she smiles at her mother with all the calm she can muster. Mama, she says, and when Katia places her hands on her mother's, she pulls them away and looks up at Martina again.

She has never stopped asking for you.

Again, Katia lays her hand on her mother's hand and this time she allows herself to be touched. Her mother's skin is like glass and Katia can feel the bones and veins beneath her fingers.

Some nights, when she wakes up to use the bathroom or because she had to go but didn't warn me in time, she thinks that I'm you. And I let her call me Katia. Because at that moment she believes you are here and the greatest sorrow of her life disappears. Who am I to tell her the truth in the middle of the night?

What's happened to her? Katia asks.

Too much loss, don't you think? She doesn't always remember Papa, but she can recite songs she learned as a child, sometimes she picks up the phone and says she's speaking to her sister and that everyone is well and that she ate such and such for dinner and that she's going out to buy a raincoat. She seems so lucid then, except for the fact that there's no one on the other end of the line.

Her mother removes her hands from under Katia's and looks at her square in the face. Her breathing is agitated and she looks from Katia to Martina several times, eyes wide, and she starts shouting in Spanish, she's one of them, she's one of them, she says, they know everything, she's one of them, she repeats. No, Mama, this is Katia, your daughter, Martina says, placing her hands on her shoulders. But their mother does not relax. From the kitchen, Martina brings a little bottle from which she shakes a few pills, turns the wheelchair around and pushes their mother back to the bedroom and then Katia hears the sound of the television, the news is on, the same news everywhere. Her mother is quiet. Martina comes back out a few minutes later.

Martina. Martina, please. How have you all been? I need to know everything.

I've thought about this exact moment every day, her sister says, her back turned. Sometimes, mostly, when—. Sometimes we were able to pretend our lives were normal, but then the smallest thing, that chair you're sitting on now, the two chairs, yours and Papa's, both empty, brought you back to this table and one of us would cry, almost always Mama. And I memorized that scene so that, one day, I could throw it in your face. But it doesn't matter.

How did our father die?

You left over twenty years ago, Katia. So many things have happened. This apartment. Martina looks at the ceiling and looks at the window and looks at the air separating her from her sister. Do you have any idea what we've been through here? I've been here *twenty years* longer than you, stuck between these four walls. And it's because you never asked yourself what would happen to me, because you thought I'd have time to get stronger after every blow, after all, I was younger, or less aware. Who knows. You thought I couldn't understand your reasons. Of course I couldn't. You took off, you left without looking back, without asking yourself what would become of me, what could happen to me. You left us here, crazed, scared to death. To death. And now you come back and want to hear what happened to our father.

Katia lowers her eyes, because every one of her sister's words pierces her body like an arrow, they fall into her as if into a dark hole. Striking the bullseye she's concealed for years under her Western clothes. Her sister is still there, willing her to yield and face the ultimate question at last, the dart Martina grips and aims directly at Katia: what happened?

Twenty years is too long. Too long, Katia. They came here just days after you left, in the evening, it was dark, and they turned everything upside down. They shoved Mama and I into a corner and knocked over the furniture. Broke glass and opened books and emptied drawers. Did you really not ask yourself? Our father didn't die in this apartment. I had to take responsibility for the papers and for his body on my own. Because he was my father, too. On my own, Katia. Your sister, the one you didn't think could understand, the one you left behind.

I'm so sorry, Martina, I swear I didn't—.

I had to piece it all together, document by

document. You, Papa, and the two of us: Mama and I, stuck here eternally. Ask Mama why we never left. Why we didn't lock the door behind us and leave all the suffering here inside. We had to wait for you, that's why. I don't believe that you have ever seriously thought about this. Did you ever stop to wonder how it was that you were even able to get out of here – Martina pauses and shakes her head and it seems to Katia that this situation pains her, but then her sister turns to face her directly. And did you really have it so badly? How many times did you ask yourself how old Mama would be, the years passing and you on the other side? You didn't consider how she would age with every winter. Or whether or not she was sick.

I did, Martina. Of course I did.

Less than a year ago, after the wall came down – Mama wasn't well already, it had been years since she was well – I was able to find out everything. They opened the archives and said, come, citizens of the East, come look and see if there's anything about you in here, orphans of the wall, and there it was, all of it, all of *us*, in old folders. They had us under their microscope for years, they clocked all our movements,

I was in there, Katia, everything that we did, they cut our lives open and stuck their hands inside. We all paid for your absence. All of us. But especially our father. Because losing one of his daughters wasn't enough, no, his punishment went far beyond that. You ask me how Papa died . . . Actually, you know what? I have something for you. Everything I've collected, everything he had. I want you to take away what I'm about to give you because it is suffocating us in here. And then I want you to leave.

Martina takes a wooden box and sets it down beside the bookshelf. She climbs up and tugs something to the edge. She lowers the old cardboard suitcase tied with string and leaves it on the table. She dampens a white rag under the kitchen faucet and returns to wipe off the dust. She leaves the now grey rag on the table. And then she breaks her silence. Do you want to know everything? Katia says yes, but Martina repeats that all she needs to know is inside the suitcase. And then she opens the door and nods her head towards the same threshold that had separated them just moments before. Katia, eyes flat with grief, picks up the suitcase and goes, but she turns back because she wants to return to the apartment and she wants to ask how their father died one more time and she wants to tell Martina that he still has two daughters, that she will care for their mother from now on, but her sister is gone and it's just the wooden door.

She passes a dark-haired boy on the stairs, about eight years old. The boy stops and looks at the suitcase and then at her. But before Katia can say a word, he has disappeared up the stairs.

When it hits Katia that she's still carrying a cardboard suitcase tied with string, one that has been wiped clean just moments ago by her sister, she finds herself standing at the entrance to the Stadt Hotel. The building had been completed in 1971, just before she left, and now it looms in front of her, its straight lines high over the lights of the Alexanderplatz. She doesn't even remember crossing the city, it had been automatic. What traffic lights, what streets? Somewhere in her brain, a deactivated map had powered up. She had been replaying the image of her mother writhing in the wheelchair, she's one of them, one of who? That's what Katia would like to know. And her sister, where was the clear-eyed girl Katia had left, where was everything else? The family she abandoned, a happy family shattered by impetuous desire. She rides the hotel elevator up with an older man. He can't take his eyes off the old suitcase. Are you from here too? she wants to ask. From here. Here.

Katia is at the door to her room. She holds the suitcase up against the wall with her leg and turns the knob with her other hand. She sets the suitcase on the bed and backs away. The silence in the room is devastating: she's alone with her ghosts in an old cardboard suitcase. She looks out of the window and can see the full length of the Alexanderplatz, its far end disappearing into the trees. Neon lights on the new Kaufhof shopping centre shine in concentric circles, the concrete serving as a canvas for the bright brush strokes, the flat roofs of the Soviet apartment blocks and the World's Clock that has been turning ever since the day their father took them to the inlaid compass rose at its base: you can see what time it is in any part of the world, girls. Katia allows the slow spin of its solar system to hypnotize her, but the same imprecise, melancholy memory releases her, abruptly, back into the hotel room. And so she turns, and there is the suitcase on the bed, still tied shut. She sits beside it, undoes the knotted string, runs her hand over the cardboard. She pops the rusted clasps and lifts the lid. She closes her eyes briefly before she sees what's inside, no longer a handful of old photographs of her parents in Spain. They're gone, the pictures she remembers from the first time she found the suitcase. Something else is in their place.

She picks up a Gilbert O'Sullivan record and the childhood memory shatters. *A Very Extraordinary Sort of Girl*. What is it doing there? The old record with the Irish singer gazing into the camera, his open shirt. She turns it over in her hands. How? How? She asks herself over and over. She sets the record on the bed and, folded in half, is the photograph of Johannes leaning against his car. His eyes challenged the camera; he couldn't know that those trips would be the only gutsy thing he'd do in his life. And there are the Elvis tape, the Neruda book, its thousands of underlined verses. It's undoubtedly her copy. Each object forming a part of a jigsaw puzzle in pieces.

The memories come and go but Katia can't hold on to any of them. The objects dimly illuminate up small spaces within herself she had considered lost to her. Mere seconds, and the light goes out again. Beneath all of that, the bottom of the suitcase is stuffed with old papers. Official documentation. Inside one small folder there are several blue delivery receipts dated from different years. *Receipt for an engraved nickel fountain pen.* Small amounts of money. *Receipt for a Trabant 601 on loan for a period of fifteen days. Receipt for foodstuffs for New Year's dinner.*

There's an attaché case containing the files of other Spaniards in East Germany. Whole trails of the lives of people she doesn't know. The eyes have been crossed out in all the photographs, a black stain: Antonio Hernández, Matilde Cabral. Names, names, names and surnames. Spanish names. She spies a small, square snapshot printed on smooth paper. In some places, the ink has worn away. She picks it up and brushes off the dust and holds it up to her face. Her parents' friends, the ones in Leipzig. The ones they never saw again. The edges of the photograph are dark, as if it had been taken through a small lens. The focus is off, as well. There they are, laughing in the garden, a big jug in the foreground. She peers even closer, and makes out Martina and herself in the background, kneeling and playing in the grass.

More papers: on many of them, someone has written that there is reason to believe this person will betray the State for some reason: they have such and such a book, they have money hidden in their home, they mock the apparatus of the State. All stamped by the Ministry. There is also a handful of keys with a little piece of paper on which are written names of various streets.

Katia picks up what looks to be a report. With a photo of her father. 17 November 1962. A letter from the committee of the Spanish Communist Party from Moscow: *He believes in the class struggle, hates Fascists, and can be trusted.* That's what is written. It's also written from then on he would be known as Informer Raffelt. A small paragraph follows that describes his suitability for recruitment. Katia tries to think back. A recollection – the two men leaving her apartment, the second man's hand on Martina's head – she closes her eyes and tugs harder on the memory and unravels a bit more of the tangled skein she has before her. Her father's long silence in the wake of that visit. There is a written statement in his own hand, declaring himself in agreement with the collaboration. He writes, her father, her father writes in German, letter by letter, that he will report any suspicion or crime against the State among the community of Spanish exiles to the Ministry of Security.

Katia picks up a handful of stapled pages. The first is dated from 1971, one week before Katia fled the GDR. She has seen these documents before. They are her false papers. There she is, her picture and that of the man who got her to the border, there it says that they are married and taking a honeymoon. The next page is a small map with their intended route. The checkpoint phone number and the names of the guards. Inside a piece of folded cardboard, more documentation.

Katia dumps the contents of the suitcase out on the bed and tosses it to the floor. She lays out the documents one by one, organizing them by date. She begins at the end: a typed letter from her father in which he confesses that his daughter, Katia, the eldest, his own daughter, has fled to the West with a man and claims that neither he nor his wife nor his other daughter,

Martina, are involved. In which he confesses that his daughter is a traitor to the State and to her own family. In which he recognizes that he was ignorant of all her plans. The letter is a report in which her father describes himself as an informant, a party militant, in which he reaffirms his ideology, in which he states that he is both Katia's father and an ally of the State and in which he begs, please, please take my record into consideration and pleads, please, for his freedom. October 1978.

Nothing that came after could hurt her as much. Her father's record of everything Katia did during the years that preceded her escape. Of their conversations. There is a photo of Johannes playing football on the other side, Johannes waiting next to his car at a checkpoint, several images from the day of the Socialist Youth, Katia dancing in the Alexanderplatz, passing by Johannes, a report on Julia recommending she be deported to Havana, her in-laws' home address in Backnang, an entire account of her life story, a report from that cold 6 January when she and her father went to buy bread.

Katia drops the papers as if they had suddenly burst into flame. She feels shame, buried sorrow rising in her throat. She can't catch her breath. She takes off her coat and breathes through her mouth. She closes her eyes and feels she's about to faint. The truth is, she wants to lose consciousness, she wants someone to come, to tell her that none of this happened after all. That her family have been fine and that she, Katia, is not guilty, she hasn't hurt them, she hasn't killed them. The other documents – the papers and lists and records – are dated prior to her escape, but the papers pertaining to her – the ones that tell of her and of Johannes, of Katia and the other side, Katia's life – are dated after she left, days after, most likely when the police came to her apartment. Her father's apartment.

Katia manages to slow her pulse, but when she opens her eyes her face is still there, stapled to all those other names, and her father is still pleading for his freedom from prison. And her mother is still on the Bersarinstraße, watching the TV, half-asleep.

*   *   *

Katia remembers all her hours in Berlin as she stands in front of the Russian stall on the Stadtbahn. She inhales the humid air, the heat hauled in from the streets and the river. Is this home? She wants to stay, then, for a moment. She wants to go back to where her sister is. Where her mother is. The home where they had lived together. She wants take care of her mother. She could follow the trail left by those years and, for her father, remember the city, for her father, raise her two girls here. Show them all the streets in the Mitte, where she could tell them, here, and here, and here. The wall, the border, the river. A necessary evil. Everything had been a necessary evil. The vendor speaks to her and Katia returns to this moment, August 1992. She looks in her wallet and takes out a five deutschmark coin and points to one of the Russian fur hats. The man hands it to her and she holds it up and sees how the synthetic fur shines in the midday sun.

She buries her nose in the hat. No, she knows. No. But still, she breathes in deep.

Poyejali.

Worldwide, more than fifteen walls that attempt to block the flow of human beings by violent means are still in existence, twenty-seven years after the fall of the Berlin Wall.

Acknowledgements

TO MERCEDES ÁLVAREZ AND NURIA QUEVEDO, who shared their memories and their *Ilejanía* with me in Berlin. And to Aitor Lagunas, who built my bridge to them. Thanks to Lara, for literature and everything that isn't literature, for that balcony in Lavapiés (with Nano, Ana, and Roberto, first readers). Thank you to David, who followed me for kilometres until I came across the scene. To my sister Conchita in her German loft, who helped me find the other side I sought. To my mother, who crossed the border with us at Mulhouse, and remembers it. And to Manfred Ziegler, for lending his name and an infinite list of songs.